"But you must have said something else to him!"

Exasperation sharpened Lauren's voice.

Her words electrified Blake. He squared his shoulders and said tersely, "The whole idea of returning the bracelet to Sheik Hassan was to get you out of a situation which could have led to serious consequences. It's about time you grew up, Lauren."

"Mr. Elliott," she said with dignity, "I'm not a child and I intensely dislike your remarks. I do, however, find it difficult to believe that Hassan would accept the return of the bracelet without some justifiable explanation."

"He had the best reason in the world," Blake replied flatly. "I told him I intend to marry you."

"Marry me?" Lauren exploded. "You must be joking!"

WELCOME
TO THE WONDERFUL WORLD
OF *Harlequin Romances*

Interesting, informative and entertaining,
each Harlequin Romance portrays an appealing
and original love story. With a varied array
of settings, we may lure you on an African safari,
to a quaint Welsh village, or an exotic Riviera
location—anywhere and everywhere that adventurous
men and women fall in love.

As publishers of Harlequin Romances, we're
extremely proud of our books. Since 1949,
Harlequin Enterprises has built its publishing
reputation on the solid base of quality and
originality. Our stories are the most popular
paperback romances sold in North America; every
month, eight new titles are released and sold at
nearly every book·selling store in Canada and the
United States.

A free catalogue listing all available Harlequin Romances
can be yours by writing to the

HARLEQUIN READER SERVICE,
(In the U.S.) M.P.O. Box 707, Niagara Falls, N.Y. 14302
(In Canada) Stratford, Ontario, Canada N5A 6W2

or use coupon at back of book.

We sincerely hope you enjoy reading
this Harlequin Romance.

Yours truly,

THE PUBLISHERS
  Harlequin Romances

Sand through My Fingers

by

LEE NAUGHTON

Harlequin Books

TORONTO • LONDON • NEW YORK • AMSTERDAM
SYDNEY • HAMBURG • PARIS

Original hardcover edition published in 1978
by Mills & Boon Limited

ISBN 0-373-02236-0

Harlequin edition published February 1979

*To my husband, Dennis —
with love,
from one desert dweller to another*

CHAPTER ONE

As Lauren Fletcher gazed at the sprawling land mass below, she was gripped by a strange prescience that the desert held her fate; that never again would she be wholly free from its spell. Deep inside a whisper stirred, a fragile intangible thing that crept through her, insisting that ever since she had been born, her steps had led towards this magic land of Arabia.

The whisper died but threads of it lingered, entwining in and out of her thoughts, making her glad that she had found the courage to leave England. She closed her eyes as the memory of the young architect she had hoped to marry made unhappiness wash over her in slow, devastating waves of pain. Once more she was drained of all emotion, a woman without belief in the enduring qualities of love, unable to accept the wisdom of the sages that time mists over the mirrors of memory, softens sorrow, alters one's perspective until, at last, one is released from pain and only scars bear witness to grief long past.

Her companion, Molly Kennedy, a good-natured Yorkshire woman in her mid-forties, studied the slender girl intently. She saw the hollows in the finely-boned face, the dark shadows beneath the grave green eyes, and she suspected that Lauren's career-girl image covered a sensitive and unhappy personality. Recognising Lauren's disquietude, she placed her hand upon Lauren's arm and said in the matter-of-fact voice the English use when they discuss the weather, 'Blake Elliott declares that the desert either rejects you, or has a fascination that holds you prisoner for ever.' She shrugged plump shoulders. 'I've never found that myself, though I've lived in the Gulf for fifteen years.' She smiled. 'If I didn't live in the Gulf, I'd live in some other

7

outlandish spot—that is if I wanted to live with Alan. Before we married, he warned me that oil is rarely discovered in civilised areas; there's always some extreme of temperature or difficult terrain to conquer before it's wrested from land or sea.' Molly grinned. 'He was right about that, but living in the oil world has its compensations.'

'So I've heard.' Lauren gazed at her new friend candidly. 'You make Blake Elliott sound interesting. I'd like to meet him. Who knows, we could be kindred spirits.'

'Oh, you'll meet him all right.' Molly's cheerful face became serious. 'The oil set-up is communal. We depend upon one another—not only for companionship and the material things of life, but also for the spiritual side, courage and hope.' Her cheeks turned pink as though she had said more than she had intended, then the moment was over, leaving Lauren with the feeling of having stumbled on an important factor, some gem of truth lying among the stepping stones of conversation.

At the airport, Lauren found it difficult to believe it was autumn. Everything was so bright that despite the dark sunglasses she wore, the harsh glare made her blink. Heat rose in waves from the dusty sunbaked ground as she followed Molly and her twin daughters towards the terminal building. Perspiration clung to her hands and face like a veneer of melted wax. Dust filtered down her throat, causing her to cough. This action, in itself, brought home to her the reality of what she had let herself in for when accepting the position as secretary to the Director of Oil Operations at Akhmar—a far cry from London and her job as secretary to the head of a small but reputable firm of international engineers.

Formalities over, she stared fascinated by the colour and contrast that surged around her. The scene resembled a theatrical setting of the Arabian Nights which seemed to have become mixed up with the cast of a modern play.

Sun-tanned Europeans clustered in small groups. Squat, dark-skinned business men, wearing lightweight suits and carrying brief cases, spoke volubly, their gestures elaborating their conversation. Long-robed Arabs, with proud, hawk-like features and sharp eyes, flocked together, their heavy scent blending with after-shave lotion, French perfume and the smell of humanity crowding together in the hot, airless room. Above this, however, another smell lingered, a mustiness that was indefinable to Lauren, but which she sensed to be an integral part of this strange land. She sniffed sharply, vaguely reminded of an attic room long disused.

Beside her, Molly wrinkled her nose. 'Now I know we're home. You can tell the smell of sand anywhere!'

'So that's what it is,' Lauren exclaimed.

Molly nodded. 'It's a smell you'll never forget, Lauren, I warn you, but to me, it means home.' She sniffed appreciatively. 'Oh, there's Alan. Come on!' With a smile and an invitation to join them, Molly and the five-year-old twins moved towards a crowd clustered near the exit.

Lauren hung back, reluctant to intrude on Molly's homecoming; besides, London office had told her someone from the oil company would meet her. She frowned. She hadn't expected such a crowd to be milling around the airport. One didn't expect it in a desert terminal, somehow. She smiled wryly. Well, it was obvious she had a lot to learn. If she stood there long enough, someone would be bound to find her.

That someone proved to be Peter Corbett. A tall, good-looking man in his mid-twenties, immaculate in a beige linen suit, he lightly tapped her on the shoulder. Startled, she turned and stared into the pale-blue eyes of the oil company representative. He welcomed her on behalf of the Akhmar Oil Company and asked if she had enjoyed the flight.

'Yes, thanks. Molly Kennedy was a tower of strength.' At his puzzled expression, Lauren explained, 'This was my first long flight, so the butterflies in my tummy were having a field day.'

'Delightful family, the Kennedys,' he commented. 'I expect you'll see them often. We're a small community.'

'I'm glad of that, Mr Corbett. It means people are treated as human beings instead of statistics from a computer.'

'Some statistics are more *vital* than others.' Lauren looked up at him keenly, but he said softly, 'Let's forget about statistics, let's be people. Call me Peter and I'll skip the Miss Fletcher part.' He grinned. 'Most of the time it's too darned hot to be formal.'

'I'd like you to call me Lauren,' she said shyly.

'Good.' Peter guided her to a shaded part of the building that overlooked the airfield. 'Wait here,' he said, smiling. 'I'll collect your gear, then we can be on our way.'

Left to herself, loneliness feathered her with relentless fingertips. Tiredness overcame excitement. The babble of voices made her head throb. The heat was oppressive. She longed for a cool drink but steeled herself to ward off the feeling of faintness. With relief, she saw Peter's tall figure.

'Sorry I've been so long,' he apologised. 'They won't offload the luggage until some urgently required freight has been unloaded.'

'Do they say how long we're likely to be delayed?'

'No.' He grinned. 'That would be expecting too much. Don't worry. I'll try my luck again, soon.'

A sudden upsurge of noise drew their attention towards the luggage bay where everything had erupted into commotion. The crowd, which had seemed a happy assembly, now resembled a tableau of frustration and confusion.

Travellers, impatient to get their luggage, were chattering excitedly to an Arab official. An elderly man stroked his chin thoughtfully and cast glances in the direction of the aircraft as if expecting guidance to come from that quarter.

Lauren looked around the airport. For a moment, sand and sky became one, blurring her vision, then she focussed, and became aware of a tall, broad-shouldered man striding towards the irate group.

Every step he took portrayed the fact that he was a man who knew exactly what he was doing. His authority was all the more noticeable because of his scruffy appearance. Khaki-drill, creased and grimy, should have lessened his impact, but as he drew near, silence descended.

With curiosity, she watched his effect on the officials. Their respect for the oilman was evident as they listened attentively to what he had to say. At last, the Arab nodded his head in agreement, then turned and jabbered instructions to the porters.

Intrigued at the efficiency of the strange European who had obtained order out of chaos, Lauren said, admiringly, 'Who is that man, Peter?'

He followed her gaze then he gave a low whistle. 'Good lord! It's Blake Elliott. What on earth is *he* doing here? By the look of him, he's come straight from the rig.'

Lauren looked at him keenly. Peter's handsome features were marred by sullen lines. Seeing Lauren staring at him, he smiled, making her wonder if she had imagined his resentment. Even so, she pondered if vendettas were easily caused in this hot dust-ridden land.

Peter said a few minutes later, 'I'm off to hustle up the baggage wallah. Stay put.'

'Don't worry,' Lauren vowed. 'I will.'

While she waited, the unaccustomed heat made her feel weak with fatigue. Perspiration ran in rivulets down her spine. Even in her most imaginative moments, she had never expected Quamat to be so hot. She passed a hand across her forehead and rubbed her fingers across the nape of her neck to help ease the aching muscles. How she longed to open some magical window for a split-second and inhale the sharp frosty air of an English autumn. Held prisoner by her imagination, she didn't see the dark-haired stranger until it was too late, and unceremoniously, she was jostled to one side.

'Can't you see you're in the way?' There was an impatience in him, an anger that brooked no retaliation, but the unexpectedness of his action, the pain of his fingers forcibly gripping her shoulders, made Lauren throw caution to the winds.

'Let me go, you brute!' she demanded. Her temper up, she rushed on heedless of consequences. 'Now I understand why drillers are called roughnecks!'

As the words hissed through her parched lips, Blake Elliott loosened his grip.

'Do you, indeed!' At his look of contempt, Lauren visibly blanched. The man continued, the words doubly effective because of the apparent control he had over his emotions. 'In that case, let's hope our paths don't cross too frequently.' Abruptly, he turned on his heels and walked away obviously to join an attractive dark-haired woman, who seemed to be waiting for him. He was followed by a black boy driving a small motor trolley laden with equipment.

Belatedly, Lauren realised if the man hadn't hustled her out of the way, she would have been knocked down. Now he was out of sight and it was too late to apologise. It was also too late to pretend that they had never met, the tingling sensation where his fingers had gripped her shoulders was an all too vivid reminder of their brief encounter.

On his return, Peter was instantly aware that something had upset her. Concern showed plainly in the perceptive eyes. 'Are you okay, Lauren?'

'I'm fine, thanks.' Lauren attempted a laugh. 'What I need is a cool shower. Can we go?'

'Certainly. Luggage has been collected and stowed. We'll soon have you settled in air-conditioned quarters.' He said gently, 'Newcomers are often affected by the heat, but they quickly become acclimatised.'

Minutes later, they were heading for the oil town of Akhmar. Relief at starting the last leg of the journey made Lauren sit quietly, the purring noise of the engine inducing a drowsiness in her that was difficult to resist. Already London seemed light years away.

Peter's voice roused her. 'If you look to the right, you can see Quamat.'

The colour of ochre, the old walled city lay shimmering in the heat haze. It stood a remnant of an ancient world and through its main gates, many camel-trains and weary travellers must have found sanctuary.

At the sight of the blue-domed mosque and minaret, Lauren could hear in her mind the echoing cries of the muezzin calling the faithful to prayer. All the mysticism of the East that had so long fascinated her crystallised in that moment.

'It's worth a visit,' Peter told her, splintering her image with words, 'but not today. I warn you though, Lauren, it's noisy, it's hot, and it smells. For myself, I prefer the westernisation of the oil site.'

'Why did you come out East?' Lauren asked shyly.

'Pay is good,' he said simply. 'And when I go on leave, I have a fabulous time.'

As he spoke, pictures formed before Lauren's eyes. How well she could visualise Peter in London, tailored to man-about-town perfection, dining at all the *in* places, accompanied by some beautiful, sophisticated creature, or lazing in the kinder sun of Cannes or Juan-les-Pins, his Nordic attractiveness and easy charm making him the centre of admiration.

'What about you?' He shot the girl at his side an inquisitive glance. 'I'd have thought a girl with your looks would be more at home in London than in this wilderness.'

'I'm not sure,' Lauren parried, not wanting to discuss her private affairs with this virtual stranger, however attractive he might appear. 'When I know the answer, you'll be the first to know.'

'Okay, Mata Hari,' he replied, and they laughed in unison, careless laughter that was carried away on the desert breeze.

After what seemed endless miles, the wheels scattering the dust over the winding ribbon of tarmac, signs of habitation increased. Shrugging off her tiredness, Lauren sat up and gazed in wonder at the size of the town that now lay sprawled before them.

After driving through a maze of intersecting avenues, they eventually turned into the driveway of a yellow brick bungalow. Lauren was surprised to see a square patch of lawn. Coral nasturtiums and marigolds made a splash of colour that was unexpected. Tamarisk trees dwarfed the oleanders which were as poisonous as they were beautiful, so Peter told her. 'What a lovely garden,' she breathed. 'And the bungalow! So English in appearance.'

'All mod. cons. included,' Peter quipped, his blue eyes amused at Lauren's obvious astonishment. 'Come on, let me introduce you to Kath. She's a grand soul.' He eyed Lauren gravely. 'Sharing living space with someone you don't like can be a problem, especially in a place where climatic conditions soon make one irritable. Kath Stevens is a sincere person, as well as a friendly one. I'm sure you'll get on.'

'I hope so,' Lauren answered fervently.

Minutes later they were greeted by a plump, dark-haired girl. Even in that first moment, Lauren sensed her warmth and kindliness, and tired though she was, she responded wholeheartedly to Kath Stevens' welcome.

After promising Lauren he would call for her the following morning and personally escort her to the office of the director, Peter left, and Kath took Lauren on a brief tour of inspection. The bungalow was larger than she had imagined—a square lounge with dining room alcove, two good-sized bedrooms with fitted wardrobes, compact bathroom with shower unit, functional kitchen that overlooked a walled-in courtyard where the servants' quarters were situated.

The dark oak furniture was company issue, Kath explained, and as all dwellings were supplied with the same basic requirements, imagination was needed to stamp the bungalow with one's own individuality.

When they returned to the lounge, Lauren sank gratefully on the settee. The air-conditioning unit was effective and after the hours spent in the heat, she shivered.

Contrite, Kath said, 'Sorry, Lauren. I should have realised how weary you must be feeling. That drive from the airport, plus the delay, is enough to make you want to turn tail and run for home.'

'Believe me, Kath, I wouldn't have the strength to get to the door.'

Kath smiled. 'I know just what you need!' Briskly, she walked to the sideboard and poured out a small glass of tomato juice which she liberally laced with salt. 'Drink this,' she insisted.

Lauren drank the tomato juice quickly, grimacing at the bitterness of the salt, glad to clear her mouth with the chaser of lime-and-lemon that Kath handed to her.

'Well,' Kath declared, 'that should do the trick. When I arrived, I felt like hell for three days. No one bothered to tell me how essential it was to take salt to replace that lost by constant perspiration.' She grinned. 'They all thought I knew! Feel hungry?—Fancy an omelette?'

'Just about.' Lauren stood up. 'In the meantime, I'll take a shower.'

After the meal, they lingered over cups of tea. Kath gave Lauren a general outline of life in the oil town. The company was generous and provided numerous amenities for its employees, including a supermarket, bakery and laundry services. There were a few local shops in Akhmar, but most people went into Quamat when they felt like a shopping spree. There was even a school which was equipped to teach children up to the age of eleven, after which they usually went to boarding schools.

Lauren said thoughtfully, 'I travelled out with Molly Kennedy. She mentioned that she'd just settled her son Timothy in some school in Yorkshire.' Her voice was quiet as she added: 'It must be a terrible wrench for parents and children, Kath.'

'Separation is an occupational hazard in the oil industry,

Lauren.' Kath leaned forward and smiled broadly. 'But once you've worked for the oil boys, it kinda gets you.'

'That I can well believe,' Lauren said earnestly. 'You've told me such a lot in so short a time, but you haven't told me where you work?'

'At the hospital. I'm secretary to the Chief Medical Officer.' Kath's face became a reflective cameo. 'I wanted to follow in my father's footsteps, be a doctor.' She shrugged. 'Big brother inherited all the talent in that field, but as medical terminology was something I grew up with, I decided to train to be a secretary on the medical side.'

'Quite a specialised section,' Lauren commented. 'Needs brains.'

'Don't know so much about that.' Kath grinned and leaned over to refill the tea-cups. 'What about your folk?'

'Father was a man who liked building roads in far-away places. There was an earthquake, and he and Mother were killed.' Lauren sighed. 'I was only five, so I hardly remember them.'

'I'm sorry.' Kath spoke sincerely.

'It was a long time ago. I've been fortunate in having wonderful grandparents. They're all the family I have.' Lauren stared into the liquid depths of the tea, vaguely aware that its anaemic colour was due to the use of powdered milk. At home, one took the arrival of the milkman for granted.

Kath spoke crisply as if to dispel any sadness that lingered at the mention of Lauren's parents. 'I can't imagine being an only child. Apart from my brother, I have three sisters to contend with. Think of that!' She glanced askance at her plump figure. 'And what's more, they're all prettier than I am. They don't have to fight the inch-war.'

'I'm sure it's not as bad as you make out,' Lauren replied laughingly.

'No, it's not,' Kath agreed. 'One thing I don't lose out on, and that's knowing the family secrets. As they never regard "Our Kath" as competition, I hear all their tales of trouble and triumph.'

A smile played around the corners of her mouth, which was large, but exquisitely shaped. She was, Lauren's intuition told her, a person who possessed that rare quality of compassion. She reflected that she was fortunate indeed to be sharing quarters with Kath Stevens.

Later, almost too tired to move, Lauren made her way to the square bedroom where she undressed and slipped gratefully beneath the cool cotton sheets.

Tired as she was, sleep evaded her. She tossed and turned and longed for slumber as her thoughts became caught up in a web of tangled dreams bordered by reality. Pictures of England filtered through her mind, memory of the flight became intermingled with the noise of the airport. Like an accompanying orchestra, the persistent hum of the air-conditioning unit lulled her into a fitful sleep. As she dozed, the face of the dark-haired stranger with the angry eyes confronted her wherever she fled.

CHAPTER TWO

LAUREN awoke early, the words of the dream haunting her. Bright sunlight penetrated the slats of the louvred shutters, casting ladder-back shadows on the colour-washed walls.

Uneasily she stirred in the strange bed and glanced around the unfamiliar room, recalling with clarity the events of the previous day; especially the mêlée at the airport. Her fingers touched her shoulders, and that instinctive movement evoked the powerful personality of Blake Elliott.

The remembrance of his anger, combined with the knowledge that she would have to meet him again and again, sent a shiver through her. In a place as small as Akhmar, there would be no place to hide. Lauren shook her head impatiently. Whatever was she thinking of? Why should *she* want to hide?

The thought of the day ahead aroused her to action and when Peter arrived just before seven o'clock, she greeted him shyly, and was rewarded by a dazzling smile.

It was only a short drive to the main office block. As they walked along the corridor which ran the length of the first floor, Lauren tried to remain composed, but the occasion was too momentous. The appointment was a big step-up from her previous job, and now she was so near to meeting her new boss, she felt breathless with excitement. Peter stopped midway along the corridor and knocked on a door clearly marked Director of Oil Operations. A decisive voice bade them enter.

Lauren felt her every sense heightened as she followed Peter, aware that her footsteps made no sound on the thick pile carpet as she walked towards a huge teak desk. Facing her was a man about forty-five. His bushy hair had a bleached appearance, his skin was brown from constant exposure to the sun, and shrewd eyes nestled in a web of wrinkles.

'Miss Fletcher, sir,' said Peter, his voice unusually subdued.

Edgar Stewart rose to his feet and warmly shook her hand. 'Glad to have you join us, Miss Fletcher.'

Feeling nervous beneath the scrutiny of the wise grey eyes, Lauren tried to speak, but to her dismay found that her voice had disappeared down a network of nerves.

The director put her at her ease. 'Please sit down, Miss Fletcher,' he said quietly, and indicated a comfortable armchair. He nodded to Peter. 'That's all, Corbett. Thank you.'

Edgar Stewart was, she noted, a meticulous man. On his desk, coloured folders lay in organised array. Three telephones, one of which was red, bore witness that this was a 'working office' despite its luxurious appearance.

'My duties?' she enquired nervously. 'Do I have any specific terms of reference?'

'Your duties will cover the normal secretarial spectrum, Miss Fletcher,' he answered. He indicated an adjoining room. 'Your office is there. You can settle in on Saturday. I presume you know that Friday is an Arabic religious day, so our working week is from Saturday morning until Thursday noon.'

'London office made that quite clear, sir.'

'Good.' He placed the tips of his fingers together in the shape of a steeple and contemplated his new secretary with a smile. 'I hope you'll be happy working for me—and the company.' The tone of his voice ended the interview, and his glance fell to his crowded desk.

Lauren rose to her feet ready to depart, when two sharp raps sounded on the door, almost as if they were a prearranged signal.

Mr Stewart smiled. 'That will be my second-in-command. He always announces his presence that way. Come in, Blake.'

Filled with consternation, Lauren watched the dark-haired stranger she had encountered at the airport walk with quiet confidence into the room.

Frozen into immobility, she stood there mentally reliving the encounter at the airport when this man had jostled her to one side. She could do nothing but stare into the cold blue eyes of Blake Elliott. The firm mouth was unsmiling. The strong face, austere. Lauren quailed. This was the man she had thought to be some roughneck!

Mr Stewart smiled. 'Good morning, Blake. Meet Miss Watkins' replacement. Miss Fletcher—Blake Elliott, the drilling superintendent.'

Blake Elliott stared at Lauren with the most direct gaze she had ever encountered. How she wished the floor would open up and swallow her.

'How do you do, Mr Elliott?' she said, trying hard to keep the ice out of her voice, but succeeding only in sounding uncertain and hostile.

'Hello, Miss Fletcher,' Blake replied evenly. 'I trust you had an uneventful journey?'

'Yes, thank you.' Lauren clamped her lips firmly together so the emotion she felt would not escape. Blake's words had been spoken with civility, yet Lauren sensed an irony in them that made her flinch. She was also conscious of his masculinity. She felt the power and the strength of the man. She looked away, but not before she had glimpsed amusement in the brilliant blue eyes. Resentment flooded through her. The wretch! He knew she was aware of his physical magnetism, and she longed to tell him, *he* needn't worry. She was sick of love and its heart-tearing ecstasies. She wanted no more of it.

Mr Stewart gazed at them with shrewd eyes. 'It looks as if you've already met. Don't worry, Miss Fletcher, you'll discover his bark is worse than his bite. Meantime, I should explain that there are two other superintendents in my department—the refinery superintendent, and the storage and export superintendent. Blake is basically a field man, and as the drilling superintendent, he also deputises in my absence. That being the case, the sooner we get used to working as a team, the better.'

'Yes, sir,' Lauren replied diplomatically. At that moment, what else could she say? Defenceless, her heart sank as she recognised the ramifications of her new job.

With a twinkle in his eyes, Mr Stewart said, 'Watkins was efficient, but Miss Fletcher is much prettier. Eh, Blake?'

Lauren was very aware of Blake's studied scrutiny, conscious that his appraisal was responsible for the heightened colour in her cheeks. The nervous note that had crept into her voice had not gone unnoticed. It was obvious that he remembered her remarks at the airport, and his eyes narrowed. 'Yes, I agree with you there, but of course, the thing is to be pretty and efficient.' He deliberately placed the emphasis on the last word.

Lauren drew in her breath sharply. Her first reaction was to retaliate, but she knew that would be unwise.

Suddenly, as if he had spent too much time on frivolities, the drilling superintendent placed an orange folder on the director's desk. 'Here's the report you asked for on Number Five,' he said crisply. 'I've covered every aspect, but when you've read my screed, there's one or two points I'd like to raise.'

'Excellent, Blake,' Mr Stewart said affably. 'Leave it with me.'

Blake nodded and walked towards the door. 'Can I give you a lift, Miss Fletcher?' he asked dispassionately.

Lauren bit her lip. How she wanted to refuse, but she could not. Curbing her rebellious thoughts, she said in a tight little voice, 'That's very kind of you, Mr Elliott.'

She felt suddenly miserable. Heat and tiredness were having their effect. With head held high to create the effect that she was utterly composed, she said goodbye to Mr Stewart and joined the drilling superintendent.

As she accompanied Blake, the thorniness of the situation

became plain. He was a senior member of the department and she had been extremely rude to him at the airport. Lauren sighed. All in all, she reflected gloomily, not an auspicious start.

As if he had mysteriously divined her thoughts, Blake spoke curtly. 'You obviously don't relish the idea of working with me, but there's no need for alarm. I won't trouble you. I'm interested only in efficiency.'

'You need have no fear on that score, Mr Elliott,' she snapped, angry with herself for losing her temper.

'I'm relieved to hear it.'

Lauren gave a sharp upward glance at the tall figure at her side, but it was impossible to read his expression.

When they reached the main entrance, she was delighted to see Peter waiting for her. Delight changed to bewilderment, however, as Blake pushed open the door, and in a voice subtle in its scorn, said to him,

'Ah, the nursemaid to the new arrivals. What would they do without you?'

'I guess we'd be lost,' Lauren retorted, and could have bitten her tongue for speaking without thinking.

A muscle tightened in Blake's cheek as he glared at them both. Peter returned his stare, and muttered under his breath. A sullen expression tautened his features, marring the handsome face.

The air crackled with invisible tension. Lauren could feel the grim, almost controlled hostility between the two men, and despite the heat, she shivered. What had caused such antagonism?

The rest of the day was a whirl of activity and information that left Lauren hot and breathless. Visiting the principal places of interest, she listened entranced to lectures on the complex nature of piping, storage, terminal and refining facilities that were needed to move the oil at a wellhead safely on its voyage. After a short film, the whole procedure was rounded off with a talk on local customs, etiquette and obtaining currency.

Yet interesting as it all was, the thought of Blake Elliott haunted her like a spectre. Now she had seen the size and complexity of the oil company's operations, only too well did she realise that the drilling superintendent was, indeed, a man of authority.

A night's sleep did wonders for Lauren's morale. As the sunlight brightened the day, so did the thought of the outing to the Arab village, suggested by Peter the previous evening, help lift her spirits and dispel the gloom which pervaded her whenever she thought about Blake Elliott.

Feeling crisp and cool in apricot-coloured cotton, she felt a glow of pleasure surge through her at Peter's low whistle of appreciation. With a caressing movement, he held her hands. 'You look gorgeous!' he told her.

'You look rather good yourself,' Lauren remarked blithely, noticing how the saxe-blue shirt and matching slacks set off his suntan to perfection, and deepened the colour of his eyes which now held a disturbing sensuous intensity as he appraised her.

At her comment, he gave a careless shrug as if he were accustomed to receiving such compliments, and the gesture irritated her.

'Enough of the mutual admiration society,' she said firmly. 'Let's be on our way, shall we?'

'But of course, my dear Miss Fletcher.' He bowed with mock formality, then grinned infectiously, causing Lauren to forget her irritation.

Reluctantly, it seemed, he released her hands, and they walked towards the car.

Soon they were travelling along the main road that linked the oil town to the jetty where the tankers loaded their precious cargo. It was a beautiful day and the scene in the distance was one huge breathtaking tapestry of blue, silver and gold, where land and sea met sky, and sunlight glittered on the silvered-steel of pipeline and storage tanks.

'You'll enjoy Maheil, Lauren,' Peter told her, turning

sharply on to a desert track. 'It's different from the oil town and not so large as Quamat.' His voice was full of animation. There was in his manner a blend of charm and confidence that made Lauren feel privileged that he should choose to spend his rest-day showing her sights he must have seen many times before.

'I hope it lives up to expectations,' she said dreamily. 'I'm looking forward to seeing an Arab village, then I'll really believe I'm living in the land of the Arabian Nights.'

'You won't have long to wait.' Peter pointed to a cluster of dwellings shaded by palms and eucalyptus trees. 'There it is.'

As they approached the centre of the village, Lauren drew in a deep breath. 'It's beautiful,' she said, thinking how inadequate that phrase must sound as she gazed at the village drowsing in the morning sun.

Groups of Arabs sat cross-legged on the ground, so intent on their conversation that they seemed oblivious of the flies that buzzed around their heads in a continuous stream.

Women, robed from head to foot in loose black gowns, their heads coifed and bound in black, walked past them with a grace of movement that a ballerina would have envied. Barefooted children laughed and chattered in the sun, or tended the goats and donkeys that wandered haphazardly, scarcely heeding the admonishments of the children or the barking of the dogs.

Lauren closed her eyes tightly, filling her mind with the tableau of mud-brick houses, the open-fronted shops, the covered bazaar and the mosque with its blue-mosaic tiles. Willing herself to remember it all so that she would be able to recall, at will, this scene that so resembled the biblical pictures Grandmother Fletcher had shown to her as a child.

'I've got to get some cigarettes.' Peter's voice was like a stone thrown into the middle of a pond, making Lauren's thoughts eddy outwards like still water that had been disturbed.

'Fine,' she said belatedly. 'I need an extra pair of sunglasses. Will I be able to buy those?'

'Wait and see what Aladdin's cave can really offer,' Peter teased, and with that she had to be content.

Moments later, Lauren gave a sigh of pleasure, finding the store a dark cave of merchandise where floral scents intermingled with the enticing aroma of foreign cooking.

In the middle of boxes, piled high on dusty shelves, there seemed to be everything on sale from scouring powder to expensive soap, dainty sandals to heavy shoes, and a motley collection of garments to fit all shapes and sizes.

From the back of the shop, a tall sharp-featured Arab glided forward. 'Ah, Mister Corbett. How are you today?'

'Fine, thanks, Ghulam. This young lady wants to buy a pair of sunglasses. Please show her what you've got in stock.'

To Lauren's surprise, Ghulam, with a smile and a flourish, produced an assortment which would have done credit to any European emporium.

Her purchase made, Lauren became caught up in discovering the delights of the store, losing track of time until Peter touched her on the shoulder.

'If you would like to see the bazaar, Lauren, we'd better go.'

'Anything you say,' she said shyly, and was rewarded by a brilliant smile.

He stretched out a hand and touched the tip of her nose. 'I'll just pay for this carton of cigarettes, and after we've seen the bazaar, what about a swim?'

'That would be lovely,' she agreed, and replacing the handbag she had been examining, she walked towards the entrance. Filled with the excitement of the morning, she didn't notice the tall figure in the doorway and bumped headlong into the arms of Blake Elliott.

'I didn't know this was a bump-into-a-rough-neck week,' he observed, and his fingers tightened around her shoulders.

At his touch, Lauren stood quite still. She could feel the

warmth of his body through the clothes he wore. Aware only of his disturbing proximity, she stifled the quiver of physical need that responded to his physical attraction, then his remark about roughnecks sank in.

Jerking free of him, she searched for some sarcastic rejoinder, but the happiness of the day gurgled through her and dispelled the bubble of animosity. 'Hello,' she chirped. 'Isn't all this fascinating?'

'I thought shopping was always fascinating to females?'

Lauren shook her head impatiently. 'Oh, I don't mean the shopping part. I mean *this*,' and with a sweeping movement of her hands, she embraced the village.

Blake said softly, 'Yes, it's a delightful spot.' He glanced thoughtfully at Ghulam's shop. 'Pity it's becoming westernised.' He shrugged. 'Inevitable, I suppose.'

'I think it's wonderful,' Lauren replied, her mind once more upon the village and its inhabitants. 'You know,' she told him, 'it's not like the twentieth century at all. Those women in their long flowing gowns don't really belong to the present.' She indicated a group of black-robed Arab ladies.

Blake smiled indulgently. 'The gowns you speak of are called *abayahs*. In many places, they're already a thing of the past.'

'And the long white garment worn by the men?'

'A *dishdash*. The headscarf is a *kaffiyeh*. One of these days, you'll have to visit the old city. It's an interesting place.'

'I'd love to go.' Excitement made Lauren lean forward, and she was surprised when the drilling superintendent stepped backwards. Bewildered, she watched him frown. Realising he was looking over her shoulder, she turned, and seeing Peter, knew he was the reason for the sudden alteration in Blake's expression.

'Here comes your guardian,' Blake said tersely. 'I should have known he'd be around.'

'Sorry to keep you waiting, Lauren,' Peter called, and

she saw his smile disappear at the sight of the drilling superintendent.

'Good morning, Corbett.' Blake's eyebrows slanted upwards in a derisive movement. 'I see you're showing the sights to a newcomer.' He smiled sardonically. 'Airing your knowledge about the desert, no doubt.' He made the statement sound like a criminal offence.

Peter turned white under his tan. 'It's none of your business.'

As if Peter hadn't spoken, Blake went on, 'One of these days you might see more of the desert than the stretch between here and the airport. Then you'll wish you did know all the answers.'

'I wanted to come here,' Lauren retorted, grimacing at Blake, angry that he should belittle Peter. A sigh of disappointment fluttered downwards. Why had there to be this discord just when Blake had started telling her about Quamat?

With assumed indifference, she smiled at Peter and linked her arm in his. It was difficult to remain unperturbed by the animosity that now charged the air. It circled the three of them—there was no mistaking it.

Lauren looked up at Blake and flushed inwardly.

As if their conversation had never been, he stared at her, his eyes cold with contempt. He was once more the arrogant stranger she had encountered at the airport. Where was the man who had talked with such warmth only moments before?

She could feel the tug of his physical magnetism, almost animal in its attraction, but she couldn't forgive him for his rudeness to Peter. With unsmiling eyes, she returned his stare.

Blake's features hardened and he gave a disinterested shrug. Without further comment, he swung on his heels and strode towards the Dodge Estate wagon, authority portrayed in his every step.

Lauren, still astonished by the lightning transformation

of the man, looked at Peter for some explanation.

He said nothing about Blake's behaviour. Instead, 'There's not sufficient time to see the bazaar, Lauren,' he said quietly. 'Come on, honey, we'll have lunch, and then that swim?'

'Fine,' she agreed brightly, trying hard not to let Peter see that the pleasure had been taken out of the day—for her, at least. She made no attempt to move, however, but stood watching Blake as he approached his car.

The Arab children who had gathered round the vehicle now ran swiftly away, giggling and chattering, but all the time watching him with wide, curious eyes.

As Blake opened the door, the girls in their long-sleeved print dresses and the boys in candy-striped *dishdasha* began to circle, then return slowly towards the car. Their bright faces showing their enjoyment of a well-loved game ... '*salaam alaykum*, Elliott *sahib*,' they chorussed.

Blake inclined his head. '*And peace be with you.*'

In silence, Lauren watched him take a handful of coins out of his trouser pocket and scatter them near the children, joining in their laughter as they scrambled in the sand for the elusive treasure.

'*Fiimaanila!*' he called. Waving goodbye to the children, he slid behind the driving wheel, lit a cigarette, then drove away, leaving Lauren with a curious sense of loss as she watched the car disappear in a cloud of dust.

'Lauren!' Peter's voice close to her ear made her start guiltily. 'I did say we'd better head for home.'

'Sorry, Peter,' she apologised. 'I'm coming.'

'Don't let Blake Elliott upset you,' he told her, his voice a curious mixture of gentleness and curtness. 'He's a difficult man.'

'I won't,' she promised, and scanned his face for enlightenment. None was forthcoming.

Together they strolled towards the car. Lauren delved into her pocket for coins, anticipating her excitement as she threw the money to the boys and girls. She was due for a disappointment. As she and Peter neared the car, the Arab children stayed their distance.

Standing like silent sentinels, the children eyed Peter and Lauren with native curiosity, but they made no friendly overtures—as they had done towards Blake.

At first Lauren could not believe her eyes. Surely the children would come? Sadly, cold realisation touched her, and she replaced the coins, despondently sliding into the passenger seat next to Peter.

Depression hovered near giving the impression that the sun had become covered by some dark cloud. With the depression came a sense of rejection. For all that Peter was beside her, Lauren knew that she was a stranger in this land she wanted to know so well.

Out of the past, the words Molly Kennedy had spoken to her on the plane edged towards her consciousness. 'Blake Elliott says the desert either rejects you or has a fascination that holds you prisoner for ever.'

Even as the statement reached her brain, she drew in a sharp breath as another sentence flashed before her mind: *What does the desert hold in store for Lauren Fletcher?*

With an excitement that both frightened and thrilled her, Lauren knew, without knowing how or why, that Blake Elliott would be there to find out.

CHAPTER THREE

MEMORIES of Blake and the Arab children at Maheil plagued Lauren's dreams. She awoke heavy-eyed when Kath called her at six o'clock the following morning. It seemed odd rising so early to start the week's work on a Saturday.

At breakfast, Kath pushed across the important daily salt intake, and Matthew poured out for her a glass of chilled tomato juice. By the time Lauren had finished a cooked meal, her spirits had revived. Over coffee, she looked at Kath with envy. The older girl looked cool and composed.

'How do you manage to achieve such a bandbox look at this unearthly hour?' she asked.

Kath eyed Lauren speculatively. 'Practice makes perfect, my girl. I've had two years to acclimatise.'

The blaring notes of a horn shattered the morning.

'Golly, Mohammed!' exclaimed Kath. 'We'd better move, otherwise he'll make enough noise to wake the dead.'

Matthew opened the mesh-covered door leading to the verandah and as they passed through it, the heat hit them like a blast from an oven. Lauren gasped.

Kath chuckled. 'You'll get used to it,' she told Lauren. 'Last month you'd have thought someone had left a shower on, too. Heat *and* moisture equals humidity, and that's the worst thing of all for sapping one's strength.' She grinned. 'Delilah cutting Sampson's hair couldn't compete!'

Mohammed greeted the two girls and opened the door of a company car. Climbing unhurriedly into the driving seat, he manoeuvred the vehicle into the stream of traffic which was already heavier than Lauren had expected. Even so early, the sun was full in the clear sky. Was it ever dull?

At the office an Indian, who introduced himself as Joseph da Silva, met Lauren as she entered the room. 'I am the chief clerk of the department,' he informed her. 'Mr Stewart asked that I should greet you and offer assistance.' As he spoke, he moved his head from side to side, and his sing-song voice hurried the words.

'Thank you, Mr da Silva,' Lauren said warmly. 'I'm sure with your assistance I'll soon settle in.'

'Please, Miss Fletcher, everyone calls me Joseph.' He added with pride, 'That is, everyone above a certain authority.'

'Then I'll do the same. Thank you, Joseph.' They smiled, glad to have found a mutual respect at their initial meeting.

Left to herself, Lauren explored the office. Compared to its English counterpart, it was an air-conditioned kingdom. Olive-green carpet covered the floor. The desk was a handsome one of mahogany sapele, with matching cupboard and bookcase. Two folding-door cabinets dominated one of the cream-washed walls. She saw to her pleasure that her window overlooked the oil town. Half hidden by the filing cabinets, a door led to a compact kitchen-cum-cloakroom. Luxury indeed!

Delighted with everything, Lauren sat in her chair and swivelled around full circle in sheer joy. She'd made it! A top job—in a top company. Whoopee! If she had worn a hat at that moment, she would have slung it in the air.

With clarity, the memory of Maheil came to mind. Blake's face rose before her—an unwelcome intrusion. His efficiency remark still rankled. She would show *him*! With that thought, she took the cover off her typewriter and prepared to master her new job.

The first thing she noticed was a handwritten message. 'Miss Fletcher, I'll be with the general manager until after lunch. Settle in, then go through the yellow folder on my desk. It lists the names and functions of the principals in my department. The names underlined in *red*—

learn them until you know them backwards. These men may want to reach me in an emergency and I want no delay as you try to place their names. The chief clerk should be able to answer most of your queries—Edgar Stewart.'

Her heart plummeted as she saw that the first entry in the folder was Blake Elliott—Drilling Superintendent. His name stood out in large block letters, underlined with a double red line. Uncomfortably, Lauren remembered she had called this man of authority a brute and a roughneck.

The morning passed swiftly. At noon, the telephone rang. Picking up the receiver, Lauren said crisply, 'Miss Fletcher here. Can I be of assistance?'

A voice she would have recognised anywhere asked if the director had returned from his meeting with the general manager.

'I'm sorry, Mr Elliott, he isn't back yet.' There was a pause and Lauren had a fleeting picture of Blake mentally chiding her for Mr Stewart's absence. She thrust the irrational thought aside. 'Would you like to leave a message, Mr Elliott?'

'No, thanks,' Blake replied evenly. 'I'll call in this afternoon. Goodbye.' The line went dead.

Lauren replaced the receiver, surprised to see her hand trembling. 'Get a hold of yourself, my girl,' she told herself firmly. 'I know it's your first day, but . . .' Deep inside, she knew it wasn't because it was her first day at all—it was her inability to rid herself of the memory of Maheil—that, and the touch of Blake's fingers gripping her shoulders.

Later, she answered a summons from the director.

'Ah, Miss Fletcher,' he said smilingly. 'Finding your feet?'

'Yes, thank you, sir.' Mindful of the double red line under the name of the drilling superintendent, she mentioned that Blake had phoned.

'When it's urgent, Miss Fletcher, Blake will come through on the hot line.' He indicated the red telephone. 'Wherever I am, contact me at once.' With shrewd eyes, he gazed at the slender girl who stood before him. 'Never be afraid to ask me about anything. Ask me twice, if need be, but be sure you understand. It's not only stupid to say you do when you don't. It can be dangerous. Time can be wasted.' He emphasised the words. 'Time is valuable. Men's lives can be at stake. Do you understand?' The smile he gave her took the sharp edge from his words.

'Yes, sir.'

'Good.' He smiled, encompassing her with the warmth of his personality. 'I trust the morning hasn't been too difficult.'

Lauren nodded. 'Challenging, sir, but fascinating.'

The grey eyes twinkled. 'Challenge routs boredom—and that can't be a bad thing.' He shook his head at the thought. 'Now, back to work. Always check for messages left on the cassette.' He handed her a batch of cables. 'The green ones have priority,' he told her. 'When you've despatched that lot, bring in your notebook and we'll make a start on the paperwork.'

After dictation, he pressed a button on his desk, illuminating the *engaged* sign on his outer door. Soon afterwards, Lauren heard the sound of Arabic and wondered who had entered the director's office.

Busily transcribing the notes, she didn't hear Blake enter the room. Aware suddenly of scrutiny, she looked up to find him standing at the side of her desk. He nodded at the red light. 'Who's with the chief?'

'I don't know,' Lauren admitted unwillingly.

The look Blake gave her suggested that she was inefficient. Provoked, Lauren replied crossly, 'Office equipment doesn't run to a crystal ball, I'm afraid.'

Blake stared at her. 'I'll wait,' he said coolly, then thrusting his hands into the pockets of his khaki trousers, he moved towards the window.

Against her will, Lauren found herself studying him. Dust covered the calf-length desert boots that afforded protection against snakes that lay invisible in the ever-shifting sand. There was a dark patch on the back of his shirt where sweat had left its mark. Her gaze travelled upwards and lingered upon the strong, uncompromising profile. She breathed in deeply, then said what had to be said before she changed her mind.

'Mr Elliott, it would seem I owe you an apology.'

Blake turned and raised dark eyebrows. 'What for?'

'Saving me from being run over by a trolley for one thing. Calling you a rough neck for another.' Lauren had the grace to blush. 'I didn't realise you were the drilling superintendent.'

A half smile lifted the corners of his mouth. 'We all make mistakes. How were you to know?' He shrugged. 'Forget it.'

'Thanks,' Lauren answered demurely. 'That's very noble.'

'Anything else you're not sure of?' he asked.

Lauren didn't answer him at once. His very presence disturbed her. His voice made her heart race. Yet had she not vowed to herself that never again would her heart rule her head? The struggle that stirred within made her sigh. With a businesslike smile that she hoped would hide the tumult within, she asked with genuine interest, 'Why are so many expatriates employed in an Arab state?' Folding her arms across the typewriter, she leaned forward to listen to what he had to say.

Blake nodded. 'Good question.' He lit a cigarette before continuing. 'Basically, it's because Akhmar is an emerging state. The local Arabs are still going through various training programmes to fit them for all the different jobs, mechanical and administrative, that oil exploration requires. Until that training is completed, others have to be employed.'

'Do you have much trouble training the Arabs on the rigs?'

'Sometimes. Muslims say their prayers five times a day, so when prayer mats are out, work comes to a halt.' He smiled wryly. 'As drilling has to go on twenty-four hours a day, we've had to devise schemes whereby prayer rituals don't hold up operations.'

'You must have many such headaches,' Lauren murmured sympathetically.

'Yes, indeed.' Blake frowned as if she had confronted him with further problems. 'There's many things to overcome.'

'Such as?'

'Getting used to new female staff for one thing,' came the unexpected reply. Unperturbed, Blake folded his arms and regarded her coolly. 'Especially redheads with flashing green eyes.'

Lauren's cheeks burned. She was about to retort sharply that it was a good job he wasn't on the interviewing panel, then she compressed her lips. She didn't want to apologise to *him* again!

Angry with herself that she should allow him to disconcert her so, she thrust a sheet of paper into the typewriter, determined to hide her feelings and let him think she was unmoved by his words.

As she watched him leaning against the window-sill, noting arrogance in the tilt of the dark head, the thought entered her mind: *Monarch of all I survey*. Rebellion stirred. She wasn't one of his subjects. She, Lauren Fletcher, was a free spirit, and any loyalty or respect he got from her he had to earn.

Lauren swallowed hard in an effort to still the torrent of words that lay captive on her lips. Rising to her feet, she crossed to the cupboard and inadvertently jerked the door open. The action brought forth a shower of papers about her feet. Standing there, knowing Blake was watching her, she seethed, determined not to let him see her dismay.

'Well,' Blake said softly, 'that's a novel way of finding out what's in the files. Rather drastic, though. Do you always start your first day in a new job that way?' He moved forward to help her, and as he handed her a folder, he said in mock sympathy, 'Hope the chief doesn't yell for something in a hurry.'

She was itching to throw something at him, but conquered the inclination, returning to her seat and banging the folders on her desk.

'Temper!' he chided. 'Destruction of company property is serious. Everything has to be imported.'

'So I believe, Mr Elliott,' Lauren replied with feeling.

At that moment the light above the director's office flicked to green. Blake glanced at it. 'Saved by the bell,' he observed. Leaving Lauren speechless, he walked towards the inner sanctum. At the doorway, he turned. 'It's a shame to tease you. You rise to the bait so beautifully.'

Looking at the jumble of papers on her desk, Lauren wanted to weep. But it was no good weeping. Muttering unkind things about drilling superintendents, she methodically started to put the papers in their correct order.

She had just completed the task when the door opened and she heard Mr Stewart's voice. 'On your way out, Blake, ask Miss Fletcher to bring me the New Construction file.'

Blake stood in the doorway. He knew she hadn't yet had time to acquaint herself with the files. Now the wretched man would have his moment of glory.

'I heard,' Lauren said to him, then taking a deep breath, she wondered where to start.

Annoyed that Blake should be witness to her dilemma, she headed towards the first cabinet.

Unexpectedly, he walked to the second one and pulled a folder out of the right-hand partition. 'Since it's your first day, Miss Fletcher, you won't have had time to know that this is where Watkins filed project reports.'

His face was inscrutable. Leaving her completely nonplussed, he walked out of the office. Confound the man! First he had stopped her from being knocked over by a trolley, now he had saved the day again. How she detested him! The thought of him made her quite mutinous.

At four o'clock, Lauren thankfully put the cover over her typewriter. What an initiation!

Back at the bungalow, she flopped into the easy chair opposite Kath. Her back seemed to melt into its curve and a feeling of sleepiness pervaded her as her tired muscles began to relax.

After the demanding day, the lounge was a refuge. The cream-washed walls looked cool, the gleam of dark oak furniture personified comfort, and leaf-green curtains blended with the bright colours of the carpet; the whole merging to make a restful background.

Kath poured the tea. 'What sort of day did you have?'

'Not bad,' Lauren replied, busily nibbling her currant cake. She realised suddenly that Kath had eaten very little. 'Are you feeling all right?' she asked.

Kath didn't answer, but moved restlessly in the scarlet wing chair she insisted was the most comfortable seat in Akhmar.

'Are you all right?' Lauren repeated anxiously.

'I guess so.' She sighed. 'Don't worry. It's just been one of those days. Everything that could go wrong did. A Doctor Massey was due to arrive today, then London cabled to say he'd been delayed, so all the Chief Medical Officer's appointments had to be rearranged.' She shrugged wearily. 'On top of that lot, the drive from the office was a nightmare. I got held up. Ever felt like a lobster being boiled alive?'

'No,' Lauren replied, puzzled. 'What delayed you?'

'Camels. A herd of them were crossing the track so I had to wait.'

'Camels! Do you see many?'

'No, thank goodness.' Kath grinned. 'Cadillacs are to-day's magic carpets.'

Lauren nodded and gazed at the *tabriz*. Kath had told her it was her most prized possession. It had, in fact, been Kath's first big buy. The rich colours leapt to the eyes.

Brilliant red and royal blue danced against a white back-ground, while threads of delicate eggshell blue, sherry brown, and greens mingled to form exquisite patterns. She bent down to touch it. 'I must buy a Persian carpet to take back to England.'

Only when Kath answered did Lauren realise she had spoken her thoughts aloud.

'Get Blake to help you choose,' Kath told her. 'If you go to the bazaar without someone to advise you, you'll end up paying twice as much as you should, and even then, you couldn't be sure you'd bought the genuine article.'

At the mention of the drilling superintendent, colour rose to Lauren's cheeks. Under Kath's scrutiny, she stirred un-easily. 'What do you think of Blake Elliott, Kath?'

'Only one word for Blake. Super!'

Whatever Lauren had expected Kath to say, it wasn't that. Before she could comment, Kath added wistfully:

'At times, I get the feeling Blake's a lonely person, but I've laughed myself out of that idea. With his looks, he needn't be. Especially with Adele Harding giving him her special "come hither" treatment. That makes him the envy of the male population.' Kath grimaced. 'Adele's the nurs-ing Sister here and attracts men to her the way flies go to honey. I can understand why Blake admires her efficiency, but to my mind, Adele's an arrogant creature.'

'A fine pair, from the sound of it. Arrogance suits them both,' Lauren muttered churlishly. She remembered the glamorous dark-haired woman who had been Blake's com-panion at the airport. Yes, arrogant was a good word to describe her!

'Hold your horses,' protested Kath. 'Don't mistake auth-ority for arrogance. Blake's a man to admire.'

At this defence of Blake, Lauren looked at her friend with renewed interest.

'Don't get the wrong idea, Lauren,' Kath said quietly. 'I'm not carrying a torch for Blake. I happen to believe that beneath that tough exterior, he cares about people.'

'Has he been here long?' Lauren's question ended the silence.

'On site about three years, but he's been in the Middle East ages.'

'What about Peter?'

'Peter and I travelled out on the same flight.' A puzzled expression crossed Kath's face. 'It's odd how that day sticks in my mind. During our indoctrination tour, we were at the gas extraction plant and Blake was talking to the shift engineer. When Peter saw Blake, he froze in his tracks.' She shrugged. 'I've never been able to find out anything, but I got the impression Peter knew Blake and received a helluva shock when he bumped into him.' She added, 'Don't think Peter will stay long, somehow. He did tell me he'd finish this contract, then seek new pastures.'

'Do you like Peter?' After Kath's comments about Blake, Lauren was eager to hear her opinion.

'Yes, I do. He's a charming lad, providing you take all he says with a pinch of salt—not to mention an ocean!' Kath chuckled. 'Has a keen eye for the girls, so don't get too fond of him, Lauren. You've been warned.'

'Is he involved with anyone at present?'

Kath frowned. 'Curious you should ask that.'

'Why?'

'Peter made a beeline for Adele the moment he saw her. As soon as he realised she was Blake's girl-friend, he changed course rapidly and headed in the direction of a pretty pert-nosed school teacher.' Kath nodded sagely. 'One thing's for sure—when the three of them get together, Adele senses there's something, and adores adding fuel to the fire.'

Lauren shook her head. 'What about the man in your life, Kath?'

'There isn't one,' replied Kath wryly. 'I can understand a buxom wench like me not having a row of admirers, but a girl as pretty as you, Lauren, surely there must be someone special?'

'Not now,' Lauren hesitated. 'There was a few months ago.' She sighed. 'Let's say the wheel fell off.'

Sensing Lauren's sadness, Kath stood up and wheeled the tea trolley towards the kitchen. At the door, she turned and said eagerly, 'What about a quick swim, Lauren, then after dinner you can show me what you intend to wear for the dance on Thursday. Be sure to choose your most glamorous gown.' She sighed happily. 'What a tonic it would be to see someone put Adele in the shade! She's a minx.' With that pronouncement, Kath left the room, leaving Lauren to wonder why Blake was attracted to the raven-haired enchantress who seemingly enjoyed creating situations.

Thursday found the two girls excitedly preparing for the formal dance which was held at the Dolphin Club once a month.

Lauren's hair, freed from the severe style she affected for the office, had been brushed until it shone. Carefully applied make-up highlighted the animation in her eyes. With care, she stepped into the chiffon gown of kingfisher blue that provided a pleasing contrast to her creamy skin and the bright hair that framed the finely-boned face. She dabbed her favourite perfume behind her ears, and after a final critical look in the mirror, went in search of Kath.

'Gosh, Lauren,' Kath said admiringly, 'you look great. You'll knock the men for six!' She smiled broadly. 'For once, Adele will realise she's up against stiff competition.'

Lauren eyed her friend thoughtfully. 'And what has Adele done to you to deserve such a fate?' she queried.

'Nothing to me, personally.' Kath shrugged. 'But she thinks enticing every male she meets is a great game. When she's successful, she loses interest, and doesn't give a fig about their feelings.' Kath grinned irrepressibly. 'But I think with you she may meet her match. You look super!'

Lauren laughed lightly. 'Thanks. Your admiration is a sorely needed boost to my ego. You look pretty good yourself, Kath. One thing's for sure, we won't lack partners.'

Kath nodded and smiled happily. 'Talking of partners, sounds as if they've arrived.'

Lauren picked up her black velvet cloak and followed Kath, joining Peter and his companion who were waiting in the lounge.

'Good evening, princess,' Peter greeted Lauren. There was no mistaking the approval in his voice. With a connoisseur's eye, he noted every line of Lauren's gown, appreciating the clever design that accentuated the tip-tilted breasts, and drew attention to the trim waist. 'You look stunning,' he said.

Peter introduced Bob Mason, a young man who had recently joined the oil company, and soon they were all engaged in easy conversation.

Night had descended swiftly. The full moon bathed everywhere in unreality and the buildings of the oil town were a collection of ghostly shadows. Strange insect sounds rasped the evening air. Dogs slunk between thatchboard fences and howled in unison with the animals that roamed the nearby Arab encampments.

At the thought of the alien world the desert became at night, Lauren shivered, and was thankful to see the bright lights of the club; to hear the voices and laughter of people.

'Lauren?' A familiar voice called her, and she was delighted to see Molly Kennedy walk towards her, accompanied by a stockily-built man. 'I've been trying to get in touch with you for days,' she scolded. 'You're so elusive. I want you to meet Alan.' Smilingly, she introduced her husband. As Lauren shook his hand, she liked the solid worth of the man. His voice was deep-throated with a strong Yorkshire accent.

The group chatted for some time, then Molly announced that they must rejoin their party. Warmly she clasped Lauren's hands. 'Now, dear, don't forget to visit us. And make it soon!'

'I second that,' Alan confirmed jovially. 'Hope we see

you before charmers like Peter book your social calendar solid.'

Peter grinned. 'Jealousy will get you nowhere, my friend.'

'I've got all the love I need, son,' Alan replied good-humouredly. He placed his arm affectionately on Molly's shoulder and they walked away. Lauren's last glimpse of them was the sight of Molly apparently chiding her husband for ruffling her hair.

Later, sipping iced vermouth, Lauren looked around the crowded scene. The colour and atmosphere created by the moving figures on the outside dance floor, the women wearing elegant evening gowns; the men resplendent in Gulf kit, filled her with excitement. Fleet-footed waiters in white tunics, their waists encircled by vermilion cummerbunds, added an exotic touch as they glided from table to table.

Peter touched her arm. 'Like to dance, princess?'

'I'd love to,' Lauren said shyly, and for the hundredth time she was reminded how easily he could devastate one with his charm. Peter proved an accomplished dancer. He guided her with expert ease and whispered endearments that flattered. Lauren knew how easy it would be to believe him—instead, she remembered Kath's entreaty not to become too fond of the handsome, golden boy.

As the music finished, Blake appeared on the steps of the club verandah which overlooked the dance floor. Completely at ease, looking distinguished in his evening clothes, he gazed around the scene as if searching for someone. Lauren thought irrationally, if only he were looking for me—then shook her head impatiently that she should have such a notion.

Peter asked Kath to dance. Lauren was glad to sit quietly, relieved that Bob Mason seemed content to listen to the music. The unaccustomed excitement, the exuberance of the band, the unusual drinks Peter had ordered for her, were making her feel muzzy. She lifted her head and the sight of Blake approaching their table made her tremble with physical excitement. Her fingers tightened around the stem of her glass. She could feel a ball of emotion gather in her throat. Why did this man have such an effect upon her? He only had to look at her, and her foolish heart started reacting with wilful stupidity. And when he spoke to her in that deep voice, either her bones melted with weakness, or she displayed a temper, she had not known she possessed. Firmly she took herself in hand.

'Good evening, Miss Fletcher,' Blake greeted her.

'Good evening, Mr Elliott,' she replied formally. 'Have you met Mr Mason? He's a new arrival—Transport Department, I believe.' Her voice was cool, but her eyes said, Be kind to him, he's not used to imperious drilling superintendents—then wondered why Blake smiled down at her.

The two men talked for some time. Lauren felt a wave of sympathy for Bob Mason. He looked uncomfortable and kept adjusting his bow tie as if he were not accustomed to wearing formal dress—or talking to men of authority. Eventually he remembered he had to make a phone call, and would they mind very much if he left them?

Blake sat opposite her, lit a cigarette, and studied her.

Suddenly shy, Lauren turned her attention towards the dance floor with its wealth of colour and movement. 'It's difficult to believe we're on the edge of the desert. It's all so . . .' she broke off, searching for the right word. Exciting didn't seem to be the correct adjective.

'Is this so different from what you expected?' Blake asked. She was very conscious of his scrutiny. 'Surely you were told that there was a social life in Akhmar to help compensate for the rigour of the climate?'

'Yes.' Lauren looked into his face. 'But formal attire seems more in keeping with a county ball than an oil club dance.'

Blake smiled. 'You haven't been here long enough to realise that this is more than just a butterfly existence. Take Molly, for instance . . .'

Lauren followed his gaze. Molly was laughing and waving

a chubby forefinger at her husband as if to chide Alan for her merriment.

Blake continued. 'For Molly, tonight is a respite from heartache wondering how Tim is settling down to his first term at boarding school. And Mac!' He indicated a red-faced, thick-set man who was enjoying a dance that one would never find in an instruction manual. 'Mac has had a dreadful day on the jetty. With tankers waiting to load, welding problems can be a nightmare. Now he's off shift, he can relax and forget the pressures of the day. And Jona-than! He's the tall man in the band, playing that clarinet as if he hadn't a care in the world—instead of working out there so he can keep his only daughter alive in some sanatorium in Switzerland.'

Lauren said simply, 'I can understand all that you say, but surely not everyone dislikes the life.'

'I didn't say that,' Blake replied evenly. 'I only pointed out that everything isn't as it seems. In a closed environ-ment, especially where climatic conditions are harsh, occa-sions such as these help release the tensions that must in-evitably build up.'

Lauren shook her head. 'Be that as it may, this whole scene seems unreal.' She shrugged, bemused. 'I feel as if I'm acting a part in some film and that tomorrow I'll wake up in my London flat laughing at my mixed-up dreams.'

'Don't let the dream finish before I've asked you to dance. That would never do.' Blake's voice was light-hearted enough, but the alert, intelligent features held a suggestion of intensity that disturbed her. He placed his right hand over hers. A strong hand that could be gentle, Lauren reflected, then blushed furiously in case he had tuned in on her thoughts. 'You're so young,' Blake went on. 'There's so much you've got to learn about life—and the first lesson one has to learn is to look beneath the sur-face.'

'You've told me why other people are here, Mr Elliott,

but you haven't told me why you came out East. Why did you?' Lauren's voice was bold and she crimsoned as she recognised the audacity of her question. The wine she had consumed earlier that evening was obviously giving her Dutch courage.

'There's an old saying that the desert calls—and if you hear its echo, it lays claim to you,' Blake replied gravely. 'I spent many of my boyhood days here. My father loved the East.' His face shadowed. 'Deciding to remarry and return to Guildford was the worst decision my father ever made.' Blake shrugged. 'On the other hand, Lauren, the Arabs have a word for it—*inshallah*.' There was no amusement in his smile. 'It means the will of Allah.'

As if the memories of the past disturbed him, he stood up abruptly. 'I came to ask you to dance. Would you care to?'

'Yes,' Lauren answered simply, and took hold of his outstretched hand.

Blake danced well. Surprise must have shown on Lauren's face for when she looked up at his, he said, 'You look as if you expected me to dance with two left feet.'

Confusion covered Lauren as he so rightly read her thoughts—then she rallied. 'In the short time I've known you, Mr Elliott, I've reached the conclusion that whatever you do, you do well.'

Blake laughed and bent his face so it was almost touching her cheek. Lauren caught the whiff of expensive after-shave lotion. As powerful as any physical contact, it made her heart hammer so loudly, she was sure Blake must hear it.

Lauren turned her gaze towards the Gulf. 'Don't you think that panorama of light is a wonderful sight, Mr Elliott?'

'Yes. Impressive. I also think it's time you started calling me Blake.'

'Very well—Blake.' Lauren's lips formed his name. Once she had uttered it, the sound echoed in her ears, and she had to resist the compulsion to say it again and again.

Unaware of her preoccupation, Blake said softly, 'And you're much too pretty to be called Miss Fletcher—I shall call you Lauren.'

'Oh,' Lauren said breathlessly, caught off balance by the unexpectedness of his approach. 'Oh, I'd like that.' She hesitated, then said quickly, 'Thanks—not only for the compliment, but for talking to me as you did earlier.' She explained. 'About people, I mean—and looking beneath the surface.'

There was an expression in his eyes which she could not fathom, yet she was conscious of some strong bond between them—some link of fate that was slowly being forged in the fire of their future. Blake Elliott, the drilling superintendent of the Akhmar oil company, was a man she would love or hate—of that she was certain. The music stopped. Lauren shook her head free of her fanciful thoughts and returned to her table walking on air.

Just before midnight, Lauren was sipping an iced fruit cordial enjoying the cool drink after the exertions of dancing a medley of Latin dances with Peter, when she glanced casually in the direction of the verandah steps.

Quickly she turned her head away, but the compulsion to stare was too strong. With butterflies racing around in her tummy, Lauren watched Blake stretch out his hand to help his companion down the steps. Instinct told her the woman could be none other than Adele Harding.

Willowy as a reed, Kath had described the nursing Sister, and Kath was right, but nothing had prepared Lauren for Adele's true beauty. She was an elegant creature wearing a crimson gown that enhanced the sleek raven hair which fell like a cloak across creamy shoulders. The colour of the gown was symbolic. Drawing men to her like a flame, then scorching them to their destruction.

With surprise, Lauren watched them walk towards their table. So conscious was she of this woman that she was only vaguely aware that Adele was smiling at Peter. With a movement that suggested a caress, she touched his arm and said huskily, 'Sister Howard is standing in for me after all, Peter dear, so I'll see you tomorrow—as arranged.'

'That's dandy,' Peter replied. He spoke to Adele, but Lauren saw that his expression became belligerent as he felt Blake's steely gaze. All too easily, Lauren understood what Kath had meant when she had said, 'Adele adores adding fuel to the flame.' The air was filled with invisible conflict. In that moment Lauren felt enmity towards Adele and silently wished that neither Blake nor Peter would be ensnared by Adele's false charm.

Realising Adele had not met the newcomers, Blake introduced her.

'Delighted to meet you, Miss Fletcher,' she said languidly, then as if Lauren's name triggered off some recollection, malice sparkled in her amber eyes. 'Oh, you're the girl Blake met at the airport.' Her slivery laugh was a bell-like sound that tinkled in the evening air. 'My dear, didn't you know that roughnecks are the most fascinating of men?'

With a struggle for self-possession, Lauren returned her insolent stare. 'Not really, Miss Harding, but then I don't believe I've had your experience.'

Colour suffused Adele's cheeks. Her feline eyes sparked with temper.

Blake stood immovable, only the scar above his right eyebrow, showing white against the sunburned skin, indicated his dislike of the conversation.

In a voice tinged with tolerance, he spoke loudly enough for everyone at the table to hear what he had to say. 'Judging by the atmosphere around here, it seems we've jumped a season and summer has come!'

'Perhaps long cool drinks would lower the temperature,' Lauren remarked, searching for the right thing to say. She was rewarded by a curt nod from Blake. 'With ice, of course,' she flashed, annoyed with herself for being affected by the unsmiling face of the drilling superintendent. *Now* there was no mistaking Blake's annoyance at her remark.

Sensing the build-up of tension, Peter spoke quickly. 'I'm thinking of taking Lauren to see Jamil Oasis.'

The look Blake gave Peter should have withered him instantly. 'Miss Fletcher has only been here a short time, Corbett. Give her time to settle in.' He shook his head impatiently. 'Anyway, you need to choose your time for Jamil. After the rains, the paths can become impassable and you could get bogged down.' He snorted derisively. 'Even on good days when the ground is dry, it needs expertise to drive over the hard windswept ruts. If you drive too slowly, it shakes you to bits. If you drive too quickly, the violent vibration of the tyres hitting the corrugations makes one liable to drift off the hard surface into the treacherous soft sand ... You have to drive at just the right speed to float over the tracks.' Blake's scorn was obvious. 'Believe me, Corbett, it's an art not easily acquired—especially by admin types.'

Blake's arrogance irritated Lauren. She wanted to say, 'Who do you think you are? Standing there, all but telling Peter what he could, and could not, do. But she knew she could not. She had to contain her temper as realisation flooded through her that this was not England. This was a closed environment where people of all levels met, on and off the job. And even as now, she was off duty, Blake Elliott was still her superior. However tartly she wished to speak to him, Lauren knew she could not do so—certainly not in the presence of others. She sighed and her dislike of Adele increased.

'I find what you say hard to believe, Blake,' Peter said airily, wine making him a little less inhibited in the presence of the drilling superintendent. 'I believe if one can drive, one can drive anywhere.'

Lauren flinched at the expression that crossed Blake's face as he listened to Peter. She took a long slow breath and said with emphasis, 'I'm sure Peter wouldn't do anything foolhardy.'

Blake's voice was deceptively quiet. 'But that's the problem, Miss Fletcher. Some people don't know when they're being foolhardy.'

An hour ago, Lauren thought unhappily, he had called her by her christian name, but now she was Miss Fletcher again. His changeable attitude infuriated her. Frustration made her clench her hands. 'Surely one has to believe in one's friends?'

'An admirable sentiment. Unfortunately, it isn't friends but the desert who decides who is foolhardy. The desert is not renowned for giving one a second chance. A trip to Jamil at this time of the year, especially with a person who doesn't know the terrain, would be foolish in the extreme.'

Blake's voice was rich and deep, each word spoken with clarity, yet tinged with a sharpness that implied the owner had neither the time nor the inclination to repeat his words.

The ensuing silence seemed interminable.

At last Kath spoke. 'It's Bonfire Night next week. Let's all keep our verbal sparks until then.' She smiled. 'Why deprive everyone of the display.'

'Now I know why I think of you as Kath the Peacemaker,' Blake told her. The smile he gave Kath made Lauren suddenly feel like a child shut out in the cold darkness of night. She sniffed inaudibly.

With charm vibrating his every tone, Blake bade everyone goodnight. He held out his hand to Adele. 'Come on, Sister Harding,' he teased, 'we'd better be going, or our friends will start organising a search party.'

Adele's eyes widened with devastating effect. 'Oh, no, Blake,' she murmured in a voice that needed no lessons in seduction. 'No one will send a search party for us.'

The inference in her words was clear. On a night such as this, with the moon gliding through the star-studded sky, the air filled with the fragrance of flowers, and the sweetness of a waltz whispering through the leaves, who would bother to search for them.

Wistfully, Lauren watched them walk away. Adele clinging possessively to Blake's arm. Sadness mingled with regret. Then as she remembered Blake's scorn towards Peter, regret turned to anger, and she wished Blake Elliott a million miles away.

CHAPTER FOUR

OVERNIGHT it had rained and when Lauren stepped out on to the verandah it was a delight to breathe in air, washed clean of dust.

The rain had swept away the musty smell and heightened the bitter-sweet fragrance of the oleanders which were over-shadowed by the tamarisk trees, some of which reached a height of thirty feet. With their feather-like foliage, it was easy to understand why the Arabs planted them as wind-breaks to protect their villages from the ever-shifting sands the winds drove before them.

Lauren had read somewhere that the roots of the tamarisk were known to spread as far as two hundred feet to find water, and she marvelled at the fact that as long as there was water within reach, the sun could not overcome the tenacity of the tamarisk to survive.

Overhead the sky was brazen blue. In the distance, a low cloud formation was gathering on the skyline. The bottom layer of cloud had turned to flame, as if tongues of fire were licking the edges, intent on devouring everything with which they came into contact. Even the sky could not remain remote from the effect of the gas flares that bore witness to man's encroachment on this primaeval land.

Yet Blake had a great depth of feeling for this part of the world. Had it always been so? Or had love for his father encouraged him to respect the primitive beauty of this tawny wilderness?

Question after question thronged one upon the other, then everything clouded as the remembrance of Adele, elegant and possessive, pushed itself to the forefront of her mind.

Lauren was glad when Kath joined her in readiness for

51

their intended swim at the Dolphin Club.

Laughter rose above the splashing of the water which glimmered aquamarine, and the animated cries of children could be heard as they practised their spectacular dives.

'Seeing those youngsters practising for future Olympics, Kath, I'm having second thoughts about swimming,' Lauren said doubtfully.

Kath laughed and dived gracefully into the jewelled water.

Uncertain whether to dive in from the side, or walk to the low springboard, Lauren stood poised hesitantly on the edge.

'Don't tell me you're one of those people who never get their swimsuits wet? I'd never have believed it of you.' The deep attractive voice made her stand motionless.

After the conflicting emotions of the previous evening, Lauren wondered whether to say Blake or Mr Elliott. In the end, she did neither. Turning to face him, she said evenly, 'No, I like swimming and so do you, I see.'

Blake looked down at his blue trunks, darkened with water, then gazed at Lauren with eyes agleam with wickedness. 'Yes, you're right. I do like swimming and I'm quite good at that, too.'

'*Touché!*' Lauren parried. 'I told you I'd reached the conclusion that whatever you did, you did well.'

Blake's muscular body was deeply bronzed. The sun glistening on the drops of water clinging to his skin made her immensely conscious of his physical attractiveness. His voice drove away further contemplation. 'After that remark, young lady, I've no alternative but to race you across the duckpond. Come on!'

'That's not fair!' Lauren protested. 'You've had a chance to get your second breath. I haven't even wet my big toe.'

'Don't sound so indignant. We can soon remedy that.'

Lauren eyed him with trepidation, and then as he stepped closer, she shook her head nervously at his nearness and instinctively dived in and started swimming. Within minutes, Blake passed her with long, powerful strokes and Lauren found him waiting at the far end of the pool.

'You've got a natural grace,' he said, then spoiled the compliment by adding, 'With patience, you'll make the grade.'

Lauren smiled sweetly, not really listening to what he was saying. She was too aware of his wet face, and how the water made his widow's-peaked hair more predominant and disturbingly endearing.

Excited cries of 'Uncle Blake—Auntie Lauren!' attracted their attention. They looked around and saw Moira and Sharon Kennedy. 'Watch us—watch us!' shrieked the twins, and Lauren realised that the twins were expert swimmers.

Lauren watched as Blake began to duck them under the water. They gurgled with laughter and shrieked with excitement, then suddenly Sharon manoeuvred and climbed on to Blake's back while Moira held on tightly to his right arm.

Water thrashed, pushing back little waves of shimmering blue that captured the sunbeams in bright irridescent bubbles, creating a web of sunlight that held them all in its golden magic.

'Come on, Lauren,' Blake cried. 'This game of roly-poly needs two a side.'

Head down, Lauren joined the fray. Caught up in the tangle of arms and legs and threshing water, happiness overwhelmed her until she became breathless.

The game finished, the twins swam away. Lauren sighed happily. Blake looked younger, more carefree, and Lauren felt herself being enveloped in a rosy glow. She had the ridiculous notion that the glow would seep through her skin and Blake would be able to see how much the simple game had meant to her. Lauren shook her head. The feeling of happiness she was now experiencing must have something to do with the sense of rejection that had been her legacy from Michael Jenson. She wondered if she would ever see the young architect again.

Too happy to dwell on such thoughts, Lauren shrugged, and turned on her back and floated down the length of the pool. The water lapped her sun-soaked skin. She closed her eyes and felt utterly content. An emotion that had deserted her for so long had returned, and she wanted the magic to last for ever.

Instinct made her open her eyes. Blake was staring at her intently as if seeing her for the first time as a woman, instead of an employee. Lauren suddenly panicked, but before she could swim away, strong hands came down on her middle and pressed her firmly under the water.

Spluttering words of indignation, Lauren threshed her way to the surface, only to find Blake bobbing up beside her. His face was alive with a vitality that aroused some inner need in her. She grew silent. She didn't want to think—to analyse—not this morning.

'Lauren!' Kath's voice covered the distance. She was standing at the edge of the pool. 'I'm going to change,' she called, and having satisfied herself that Lauren had heard her, she walked towards the clubhouse.

'I think I'll do the same,' Lauren told Blake.

He nodded and pointed to some seats on the lawn-covered terrace that surrounded the far side of the pool. 'I'll join you there,' he said softly. The smile he gave Lauren made her tremble.

After changing, Lauren made her way to the spot Blake had indicated and giving a sigh of pleasure, she settled herself comfortably in a deck chair.

'Enjoy the frisk in the pool?'

Lauren looked up, pleased to see Molly Kennedy.

'It was fun,' she smiled.

'I'm glad you enjoyed it. The twins go berserk when they see Blake and tend to get out of hand.'

Lauren nodded understandably. 'I didn't know children could swim so well,' she remarked with feeling. 'Your five-year-olds make me feel like an amateur.'

'Nonsense,' Molly retorted, settling herself beside Lauren. 'Anyway, Lauren, I didn't come here to talk about swimming, but to invite you to dinner tonight. Can you come?'

'I'd love to,' confessed Lauren, and smiled at the older woman. 'One thing I can't get used to, Molly,' she went on, 'is the way the children call me Auntie. Your relations must wonder at the number of adopted relatives your children possess.'

'Oh, they're used to it.' Molly looked fondly at her off-spring, now playing in the nearby sandpit. 'Blake is their godfather,' she told Lauren. 'They adore him.' She sighed resignedly. 'He spoils them disgracefully.'

Lauren nodded her head and smiled at the thought of the twins' subject of adoration. 'Have you known Blake long?' she asked Molly, filled with a sudden desire to learn all she could about the drilling superintendent.

'We've known Blake for years,' Molly confided. 'He and Alan were at El Rubai at one time. It's grand meeting up in Akhmar.' Her face became grave. 'That's the trouble making your home overseas, Lauren. You make many friends, but sooner or later people move on. It's impossible to keep in touch, however hard one tries.'

'Yes, I'm sure it must be,' agreed Lauren. 'How's Timothy?' she asked warmly, remembering Molly's son who had had to remain in England.

'Oh, he seems to be settling down.' Molly sighed. 'Reading in between the lines, a bit homesick, I'd say.' A film of maternal anxiety clouded her eyes. 'Going to boarding school at eleven is a big adjustment, even if your family is near. Over two thousand miles away—well, it's a wrench.' She grimaced. 'For the mother as well.'

'It must tear you in two, Molly,' Lauren murmured sympathetically.

'I'll survive. I come from a hardy breed, which reminds me I must go and gather up my brood.'

'What time shall I come tonight?' Lauren asked shyly.

'About six-thirty. No need to be formal.' Molly stood up and looked at the pretty girl in the deck-chair. 'I must say you cut a dash at the Dolphin last night. More than one young man asked me who you were.' She raised her eyebrows. 'I told them to find out for themselves—so don't forget to answer your phone. 'Bye!'

Lauren lay back in the deck chair and closed her eyes. She felt at peace with the world. Life was heavenly, sheer bliss. Why had she waited so long to start living again?

'The Sleeping Beauty in a deck chair!' Blake's voice was light as if he was enjoying Lauren's discomfiture at finding him staring at her.

The morning must have had a benevolent effect upon him, too, Lauren thought. She studied him as he sat in the deck chair beside her. How different people look with their eyes closed, she reflected.

As if sensing Lauren's gaze, Blake opened his eyes. 'How old are you?' he asked her unexpectedly.

Taken off guard, Lauren replied automatically, 'Twenty-four.'

'You look younger than that.' He studied her intently, then observed casually, 'Ed Stewart is right—you're definitely prettier than Watkins.'

Lauren blushed and sat with her hands clasped in her lap. 'How old are you?' she asked impetuously.

'Thirty-five.'

She drew in a deep breath. 'Have you ever thought of marriage?' She shrugged, amazed at her temerity.

He nodded casually. 'I believe everybody thinks about marrying as they go through their teens and twenties. I was no exception.' He yawned. 'Now they point me out as a confirmed bachelor.' He raised dark eyebrows. 'What about you?'

Lauren didn't want to answer him, but was caught in a trap of her own making. 'I nearly got engaged last year, but things didn't work out.' She lifted her eyes to meet his, and felt embraced by the all-seeing look that conveyed he knew what unhappiness could do to people. Lauren turned away quickly, but Blake stretched out his hand and touched her arm with gentle fingers.

'You have such a white skin, Lauren,' he said unexpectedly. 'You must be careful not to become unduly exposed to the sun. It can be harmful.' The calmness of his voice soothed her. 'Buy yourself one of those floppy hats to protect the nape of your neck,' he advised.

At his words, Lauren's hand strayed to her hair.

In mock severity, Blake brushed her hand aside. 'Never mind about a hat spoiling your hair-style. Nature has a wonderful way of making us get our priorities in order.'

The gentleness in his voice confused Lauren. Was this the arrogant man she had met at the airport, and at Maheil? Was this the autocrat who spoke to Peter with such scorn? Instinct told Lauren that beneath Blake's harsh exterior, lay another man—a man who was too attractive by half for Lauren Fletcher's peace of mind.

The idea made absurd notions go spinning around in her head. She reached down to pick up her handbag. Blake was much too near for comfort and she didn't want him to interpret any expression he saw on her face. With relief, she heard Kath's voice.

'I'm sorry, Lauren,' Kath apologised. 'I didn't mean to desert you, but I've just met that new doctor. He's super!' She stopped abruptly. 'Oh, hello, Blake,' she said bashfully.

'Hello, Kath,' Blake answered, half-smiling. 'I heard a new medic was arriving. What do they call him?'

'Edward Massey.'

'The name rings a bell. Massey, you say?' Blake frowned. 'No, I can't place him at the moment.'

Kath glanced at her watch, then at her friend. 'Lauren,' she said quickly, 'Ted, I mean Dr Massey, is coming to the photographic meeting this afternoon. That starts at two-thirty, so we'd better go for lunch.'

'Okay,' Lauren replied, and gazed at Kath in some surprise. Her usually placid face was flushed with suppressed excitement. She sounded breathless as if she had just run a hundred-metre race. This new doctor must be quite a man, Lauren thought, to knock 'our Kath' off balance at first meeting.

'Would you like to join us for lunch, Blake?' asked Kath. 'Matthew does a superb curry.'

Lauren murmured, 'I can vouch for that.'

Blake nodded and smiled. 'I'd love to join you ladies for lunch, but I've another appointment. I've also promised to play tennis. Another time, perhaps?' He gave the impression that it was his loss. He stood up swiftly, and stretched out his hand to help Lauren to her feet.

At his touch, she felt a sudden dryness in her throat. His face was so close. His nearness induced a physical awareness that was not to be encouraged.

To her relief, he stepped backwards, then with a casual movement stopped to pick up her towelling robe that had slipped unnoticed to the ground. As she took it from his grasp, the simple action restored her composure and she said calmly, 'Thanks, Blake. I enjoyed the swimming.'

As she and Kath headed for home, a murmur of discontent stirred in Lauren's heart. Was Blake's appointment with Adele?

Over lunch, Kath was unable to contain her excitement. Her meal remained almost untasted as she relived the morning's encounter.

'How old is this Dr Massey?' Lauren enquired patiently.

'Late twenties, I would think.' Kath went on dreamily, 'He isn't handsome like Peter or devastating like Blake, but he triggers off my chemical reactions.'

'You don't say,' Lauren said dryly. They both laughed.

'What about you and Blake?' Kath asked quizzically. 'From what I saw this morning, you appear to have reached a truce after the sparks that were flying last night.'

'I can't make the man out,' Lauren said casually. 'After last night's lecture on how one drives in the desert, plus his antagonism towards Peter, I was furious. I never wanted to see the wretch again!' She sighed audibly. 'I decided to keep my cool at all costs—and also keep *him* at a distance.' Lauren shook her head confusedly. 'Yet after this morning, I found myself wishing Blake had accepted your invitation to lunch.' Her voice became studiedly blank. 'I expect he's lunching with Adele.'

Kath looked surprised. 'I don't know what gave you that idea. Didn't Peter tell you last night that he had a new arrival to meet this morning, so he agreed to drive Adele to the airport!' She shrugged. 'She's going to Beirut. She must like the social climate—she goes there often enough.'

Lauren tried not to think about Adele and Peter. The memory of her husky seductive voice and her possessive touch of Peter's arm made her feel distinctly uneasy. Was it this relationship that lay at the root of Blake's antagonism? Lauren sighed. She liked Peter, and she didn't want to see him hurt, and somehow caught between Blake and Adele— she couldn't see him escaping lightly.

'Having met Adele, what do you think of her?' Kath asked casually.

'Beautiful,' Lauren declared. 'I suppose she's popular,' she added in a matter-of-fact tone.

'With the male population, undoubtedly. With the female, it's debatable.' Kath frowned. 'To be honest, Lauren, I find Adele's an enigma. Off duty she appears to be such a butterfly—on duty she's the reverse. Her ward runs like clockwork. The doctors admire her. The patients trust her, and that's important, even though she tends to treat them as case histories instead of people.' She shrugged, perplexed. 'My father would say she lacks the essential factor— compassion. I just don't know.'

Lauren toyed with her spoon, then she said, 'Do you think Adele and Blake will marry?'

Kath's eyes narrowed. 'Adele likes to make people think they will, but I've my doubts.' She shrugged. 'Call it feminine intuition if you like.'

Later that evening Lauren walked the short distance to the Kennedy bungalow.

'Glad you could come, Lauren.' Molly's face was bright with a welcoming smile. 'Make yourself comfy,' she said, pointing to the settee. 'I'm just reading the twins their bedtime story before the nursemaid settles them for bed. I won't be a jiffy.'

Settling herself in the seat Molly had indicated, Lauren examined the lounge with interest. As Kath had told her, all bungalows were fitted with the same basic requirements—but here, in this room, a family unit had been created, it showed in the cushions and brightly-coloured paper flowers made by Molly, her knitting laid on a side-table, jigsaws and childrens' books near a man's pipe and tobacco pouch—all these betokened a home.

When Molly returned, her face was soft and maternal. 'I wish I'd half their energy,' she said, as she flopped beside Lauren. 'Years in this climate does sap one's reserves.' She studied Lauren thoughtfully. 'How's the job?'

'Wonderful,' Lauren said happily. 'Mr Stewart is a charming man. In time, I might be able to say the same about Blake Elliott.' Quickly, she clapped a hand over her mouth. She hadn't meant to say that at all.

Molly didn't miss the gesture. She gave a burst of laughter as she listened to Lauren's impulsive remark. 'First impressions aren't always right, Lauren.' Her voice was warm and friendly. 'Forget about the gaffe at the airport.'

'How did you know about that?'

'Oh, the bush telegraph in Akhmar is extremely efficient. It's more reliable than the telephone system.'

'That being the case, you know Adele wasn't overjoyed to meet me last night?'

'Adele Harding only likes women who are dowdy and dull, so I wouldn't let her lack of enthusiasm worry you.'

'I won't,' Lauren said quietly.

Molly eyed her speculatively. 'What's bothering you, Lauren? Care to tell me?'

'There's nothing to tell.' Lauren tried to sound impersonal, but it was easy to see Molly wasn't convinced. The warmth of the older woman's presence, her sympathetic gaze, made the girl feel the urge to unburden herself. She sensed by talking to Molly, she could sort out her mixed-up thoughts about the enigmatic drilling superintendent. 'I find Blake Elliott such a complex man,' Lauren started to say.

'In what way?'

'Difficult to describe. One minute he's so arrogant, I'd like to throw something at him. The next, he's positively charming.'

Molly said sincerely, 'We're fond of Blake. Alan admires him tremendously.' She chuckled. 'He says Blake brings out the best in men—even though they do call him a slave-driver!' Her face became grave. 'Apart from having the highest regard for his technical ability, they know he works as hard as they do. And furthermore, his presence during the many tricky problems that can crop up on a drilling rig inspires them with complete confidence.'

'How long have you known Blake?' Lauren asked.

'About nine years. Alan had been taken into hospital with appendicitis and Blake was brought into the same ward.' Her expression altered as she remembered the occasion. 'There'd been a rig fire. Believe me, Lauren, they can be highly dangerous.' She sighed audibly. 'That one certainly was! Blake was a hero. Dr Frost said it was a miracle that Blake wasn't burned to death. Eventually, he and Blake became good friends. They meet from time to time in Beirut, I believe.'

'Was Blake in hospital long?' asked Lauren.

'A fair number of weeks in Beirut, then he went to England for further treatment. The only visible sign that the accident ever happened is the scar above his eyebrow.' Molly shook her head reflectively. 'In a way, Lauren, I suppose that's why you keep seeing two sides of Blake. The job side demands that he be as hard as nails, physically and mentally, a human robot who can't allow weakness or personalities to affect his judgment, yet he has to remain a human being.' She studied Lauren's face. 'Few people ever see Blake completely relaxed.'

'That explains a lot, Molly. Thanks for telling me.' Then Lauren thought of something else. 'What I do find difficult to understand is Blake's animosity towards Peter Corbett.'

There was silence and, for the second time that evening, Lauren realised she had spoken imprudently.

The sound of a car approaching the bungalow dispelled the awkward moment. The clang of the doors being slammed made a metallic noise that reverberated in the night. Footsteps sounded on the concrete path and with pleasurable surprise, Lauren recognised the voice of Blake Elliott.

Molly opened the door. Alan, dressed in tennis kit, was accompanied by Blake, who in sharp contrast to Alan's casual wear, was attired in grey-tailored slacks and a wine silk shirt.

Lauren felt very conscious that her heart was beating rapidly; her pulse was racing, and she was trying to recollect if Molly had mentioned that Blake had been invited to dinner. Vaguely she was aware of Molly and Alan talking, then she heard Molly address Blake.

'Lovely to see you, Blake. I'm so glad you could make it.'

He smiled and kissed her lightly on the cheek. 'How's my best girl?'

'Better not let the twins hear you call me that—they think they've first claim on you!' Smiling, she turned to her husband. 'Did you have a good game, dear?'

'Yes, but as usual, Blake won.' Alan's voice held no rancour. He was stating a fact. 'Hello, Lauren,' he greeted her. 'My, my, you look as pretty as a picture—doesn't she, Blake?'

'Delightful,' Blake replied. Lauren was very conscious of

his eyes upon her. She had the feeling that Blake was seeing beyond her outward appearance and was discovering the knowledge that lay within her. Suddenly she didn't want him to know too much about her. Such knowledge would make her vulnerable. She shrugged off the fanciful notion, and smiled brightly. 'Thank you, both,' she said sincerely. 'Such compliments can do wonders for a girl's morale.'

'You don't look as if you need your morale boosting,' Blake observed.

Noticing his immaculate appearance, Lauren retorted saucily, 'And you don't look as if you've been playing tennis.'

'Appearances can be deceptive,' Blake answered, his voice pleasant, half amused.

To Lauren's astonishment, Alan winked at her. 'The ball's in your court now, Lauren,' he told her, and with that comment, he went to change.

Molly glanced at her watch. 'Now, you two, you must excuse me—I have to see how things are shaping in the kitchen. Play host, Blake. You know where the drinks are.'

Blake nodded and smiled, then said crisply, 'What would you like, Lauren?'

'Dry Martini, please.'

'Stirred or shaken?'

'Is there any difference?' Lauren asked naïvely.

'My goodness,' Blake replied, 'we've got a job on with this girl!' He inspected the contents of the drinks cabinet and said conversationally, 'Did Kath enjoy her meeting?'

'She certainly did,' Lauren replied. 'I'm anxious to meet this Doctor Massey.' She said wistfully, 'I only hope he lives up to expectations. I wouldn't like Kath to be let down. She's a genuine soul, and you don't meet many of *those* these days.'

'Charming,' Blake retorted, misinterpreting her words. 'We are as life has made us,' he pointed out.

For a moment, the air between them became charged with the forces of their individual personalities; their eyes met—and held. The light from the chandelier glinted on Blake's dark hair, emphasising the deep-set eyes which now hypnotised Lauren into silence, and the moment became a fragment of time that imprints an image on the memory that is never erased.

'Did you remember where you'd heard the name Massey?' Lauren asked in an attempt to hold on to her composure. Blake's nearness was doing strange things to her metabolism.

'No,' Blake replied, 'but I'm sure I've heard the name.' He stared down at her; his expression inscrutable. 'Now, what about those drinks?'—the clink of glasses finally dispelled the subtle spell that had bound them.

After a well-cooked meal, Lauren sat bemused, content to listen to Blake talking to the Kennedys. The aroma of cigar smoke tantalised her nostrils and she knew it would always remind her of this magical evening. She need never wonder what it would be like to be transformed from a Cinderella to a princess. She knew—and was grateful for the gift.

With that rapport that existed between them, Blake must have sensed her thoughts about the midnight hour, because he stood up and said regretfully, 'It's almost twelve, young Lauren.' He shook his head as if warning her what happened to people who were out after the witching hour. 'Come on,' he said softly. 'Tomorrow is another day. I'll drop you off at the bungalow, then I'll head for home.'

As he opened the door of the Dodge estate, Lauren stared at the far horizon, fascinated by the red glow that coloured the sky.

'Gas flares,' Blake told her.

'I know,' Lauren whispered. 'I look at them every night and wonder what they must be like close to.'

'Would you like to see them?'

'I'd love to.'

'Now?'

'If it's not too late?'

Soon the oil town was a speck in the distance. As they drove past the tank farm, the monster steel storage tanks glistened in the moonlight, giving Lauren the impression that earth was far away and they were now entering an unknown world. The further they drove, the more pronounced became the feeling of eeriness that the desert evoked at night. Stars glittered silver in the velvet sky and the light from the moon cast unfamiliar shadows on the landscape. On either side of the hard track lay expanses of gravel and soft sand. The escarpment lay silhouetted on the horizon like some huge mythological creature guarding the land.

Lauren drew in a deep breath. Out there lay the deep silent desert. Was it laying its claim to her? The thought awoke strange longings in her, causing excitement to rise as if the very winds of the desert were playing their haunting melody upon her heart-strings. She glanced sideways at Blake. His profile, dark and expressionless, heightened her awareness of his physical nearness. She felt a strong desire to touch him—caress, almost—and her cheeks crimsoned at the mental picture she was creating.

Blake's voice, close to her ear, startled her. 'Is this your first glimpse of the desert at night?'

'Yes,' Lauren said quietly, hardly trusting herself to speak. 'It's awe-inspiring.' She paused, as if trying to find the exact words that would convey her feelings. At last she said, 'It's so vast. It makes man's efforts seem puny, somehow. It's majestic.'

Blake studied her for a moment. 'I think you understand why men say the desert possesses a beauty all its own. It also has strange moods.' His smile was sombre. 'One has to understand the desert to survive. It's magical and merciless and eternal.'

'You sound poetical.' Lauren's voice was the barest murmur.

'The desert has inspired great poetry and prose. Its very timelessness makes men look inside themselves—thus mys-

tics are born.' He glanced at her. 'You should read some of
the writings of Kahlil Gibran. I'll let you have one of his
books—then perhaps you'll understand what I'm trying to
say.'

'I think I do anyway. I've read *The Prophet*. I'd certainly like to read others. Thanks . . .'

Lauren's thanks were cut short as the headlights picked
out a large spiny-tailed lizard as it ran across the road.

The terrain became more rock-strewn and patches of
scrub grass were phantoms on the moon-washed night.

After they had driven about fifteen miles, Lauren was
aware of a curious odour. 'Ugh! Whatever is that smell?'

'Sulphur.'

'More like rotten eggs.' Lauren wrinkled her nose. 'I
never thought such a smell could be so overpowering!'

Blake inclined his head. There was a gleam in the dark
eyes. 'Do you want to turn back?' His question was almost
a challenge.

'No, but I'm glad there's such things as French perfume.'
Quickly she groped for her cosmetic purse. 'Where does the
gas come from, and why does it have to be burnt off?'
Lauren enquired. Now she had come this far, she might as
well be told what it was all about.

'In with the oil, there's always gas,' Blake explained. 'If
it weren't separated and burnt off, there'd be a pressure
build-up and explosions would occur.' He nodded gravely.
'Even if these flares went out for a short time, it would be
dangerous.'

'I didn't realise that.'

Lauren gazed upon the strange area of unreality that resembled some sterile lunar landscape and caught her breath
with the wonder of it all. The sky looked like a scarlet
backcloth for Dante's Inferno, all the more impressive because of the brooding menace of the wasteland.

Blake stopped the car and helped her out.

Suddenly aware of the distant roar of flames, Lauren

trembled, glad when Blake held her hand in a reassuring gesture.

'Look at that sky,' he said, his voice filled with something akin to awe. 'Look at those stars twinkling a million light years away, completely indifferent to man. Yet it produces a wonderful effect. Don't you agree?' He looked down at the slender girl whose hand was gripping his own so forcibly. Lauren nodded tremulously, overcome by the wonder of it all.

Blake's face became remote as he studied the heavens. 'The only other thing I know to beat it is the sense of solitude one finds in the deep desert.'

'It's fantastic,' she said, but inside a thousand words lay stillborn. How could she explain the myriad emotions this visit was stirring in her heart? It was so unlike anything that Lauren had ever experienced that its primitive magnificence overwhelmed her.

'Well, now I've brought you this far, let's go nearer to the flares.'

'You're the boss,' she said, holding his hand tightly.

With slow steps, they walked towards the line of flames which seemed to set the sky on fire. The heat was tremendous. Lauren's face was tender, yet her back was strangely cold from the night air.

As if released from the earth, and glad to have escaped, the flares stretched up tongues of fire to lick the heavens. The noise was deafening. As she stood watching the man-made inferno roar heavenwards, the thought occurred to Lauren that she was alone with Blake, utterly alone, and yet as he smiled at her, another facet of the man became known. She could so easily have felt afraid, yet fear did not touch her because she sensed he was a man she could trust completely.

Without speaking, they retraced their steps towards the car. When they reached the vehicle, he bent his head forward and there in that tremulous moment, Lauren thought he was going to kiss her, but instead his fingers traced her cheek. He said, 'Lauren Fletcher, do you know you're the most infuriating, tantalising, endearing female I've ever met? My life has never been the same since you arrived on site.'

With an abrupt gesture, he straightened his shoulders and opened the car door. 'It's late. I'm taking you back to quarters.'

Lauren glanced backwards at the flares, at the taut figure and enigmatic profile of the oil man, and knew that this night would be imprinted on her memory with indelible vividness: the night—and Blake Elliott.

CHAPTER FIVE

WITH a sigh, Lauren closed her Arabic textbook and once more tried to pronounce the awkward-sounding phrases, only to be greeted by a roar of laughter.

Startled, she glanced up and saw Blake leaning against the jamb of the office door.

'Come, come, Miss Fletcher,' he mocked. 'Surely you can do better than that?'

'What's wrong with it?' she demanded defensively.

'You only introduced yourself as *the son of your father*!' He laughed. 'I'm glad you're not—biologically speaking, I mean. To tell you the truth, I think you're *inta jamil*.'

For a moment she was at a loss. Then, 'It's kind of you to call me beautiful,' she replied demurely.

Lighting a cigarette, he said easily, 'Let's revert to the original topic of conversation. Don't get mad at me, but your Arabic pronunciation is diabolical.'

'I know,' Lauren said unhappily. 'And with the exam only a few months away, I'm still tackling the greetings.'

He moved nearer and sat on the edge of her desk. 'Don't underestimate the importance of the greetings, Lauren. The Arabs set great store by them.' He drew thoughtfully on his cigarette. 'Having a conversation with them is never straightforward. There they sit and click their amber worry beads and enquire about the health of the whole family before they'll discuss any matter, however important it may be.'

He bent over her and tapped the phrase book. 'So remember, young Lauren, you won't get anywhere unless you master the formalities of the greetings.'

'Thanks, Blake,' said Lauren, listening to him carefully,

but finding it difficult to concentrate on what he was saying to her. Clad in khaki shirt and trousers that were streaked with oil and sweat, looking distinctly masculine, his physical presence once more aroused that spark of desire she was trying hard to suppress. As he stood up, his shoulder brushed her face and all too vividly she recalled the touch of his arm about her shoulder as they had gazed at the flares.

Mentally chiding herself for succumbing so easily to his charms, she drew in a deep breath in an effort to dispel the band of emotion that was threatening to suffocate her. She said crisply, 'Mr Stewart is visiting the Sheik with the general manager.'

'I know,' Blake replied seriously. 'That's why I'm here. The chief phoned me earlier.'

A sudden movement in the next room brought Lauren to her feet, but Blake strode before her and briskly opened the door of the inner sanctum. She heard Mr Stewart say, 'Ah, Blake, come in. Tell Miss Fletcher to hold the fort—I don't want to be disturbed.'

Almost as if everyone knew the director had returned, the office suddenly became very busy. Lauren was busy sorting out travel documents when Peter telephoned.

'Hello, honey,' he said, his voice oozing charm and sex-appeal. 'Will you join me for dinner tonight?'

'That's what I call a delightful suggestion,' Lauren answered gaily.

'Wear something extra pretty,' Peter urged. 'I'm taking you out to celebrate.'

'Your birthday?' she enquired.

'No. I'll tell you tonight,' he replied mysteriously. 'Be ready at seven.'

'On the dot. I must ring off now—things are busy.'

Lauren had just replaced the telephone receiver when the buzzer sounded, and smiling, she entered the director's office.

Mr Stewart glanced at the air tickets she had organised.

'I should be back from London within a fortnight,' he told her. 'Then it will be Blake's turn for a stint in the big city.' His eyes twinkled. 'That is if we can persuade him to leave all this behind.' He smiled. 'During my absence, Blake will be holding the reins. I've told him not to run you off your feet, but be warned, Miss Fletcher—he's a slavedriver even though he has a light touch with the whip.' Chuckling at his little joke, he indicated the *out* tray, then glanced at his watch. 'Deal with that lot, then call it a day.' He beckoned to the drilling superintendent, who had been listening to the comments about him with a half-amused smile. 'Come on, Blake, I've still got a lot to do.'

Clutching a mountain of papers, Lauren wished Mr Stewart a good trip, then headed for the door. Blake reached it before her and swung it open with a flourish.

'*Fiimaanila*, Miss Fletcher,' he said softly, and there was a wealth of meaning in the familiar voice.

Lauren's heart lurched, and as she wished him goodbye it crossed her mind that her Arabic might well improve within the next fifteen days.

Peter arrived at the bungalow at seven o'clock, and Lauren could tell at a glance that he was in a festive mood. 'Hello, honey,' he greeted her. 'Anyone ever told you that your face and figure are your fortune?'

'In that order, would you say?' she replied flippantly.

'Perfect in every way,' he said as he took her hands and kissed her lightly on the forehead. 'Mmm! That perfume has impact. For my benefit, I presume?'

'If you choose to think that, why should I disillusion you?' she teased.

'Magnanimous of you,' he told her, giving a mock bow. 'However, Lauren, just to show you're my favourite girl, I'll treat you to a champagne cocktail. Show you how the rich live.'

'Thank you, kind sir.' Lauren curtsied, then wrinkled her nose impishly. 'I'm all in favour of further education,' she said pertly, and smiled up at him, thinking to herself that life was suddenly terrific.

A little later they were sitting in the cocktail bar of the Dolphin Club, sipping the champagne laced with brandy. The sybaritic sensation of tasting the frosted sugar decorating the rim of the glass was a new one to Lauren. She smiled at Peter. He looked attractive with his blond hair well groomed, and his bronzed skin contrasting with his white sharkskin suit. Little wonder girls went overboard for him!

Emptying her glass regretfully, she placed it on the bar top. 'If this is how the rich live, I'm all in favour,' she told Peter, and smiled happily.

'You're just a beginner. One cocktail is enough for starters.' He grinned. 'Any more and you'll be seeing double cutlery.' Ignoring Lauren's pretended moue, he took her hand and pressed his fingers into her skin. There was a suggestion of intimacy in his touch that Lauren could not ignore.

She moved restlessly. 'Let's eat,' she suggested, feeling the dining room was a good place to keep things in perspective. Choosing meals stopped one's passions getting out of hand. That is, a wicked voice inside whispered, if you didn't want them to be aroused—and for a moment she thought of Blake Elliott.

'I don't feel like eating yet,' Peter remarked. 'Let's stroll.' He smiled. 'A walk by the swimming pool would be pleasant, don't you agree?'

'With moonlight thrown in as a bonus,' Lauren retorted blithely. What chance did a girl have against champagne, moonlight and a dishy escort like Peter Corbett? She breathed a gossamer sigh.

Peter shrugged in jest. 'Sorry, I can't provide the Taj Mahal.'

Lauren laughed at his expression, suddenly very happy to be teased and filled with a renewed zest for living that she had never thought possible until yesterday.

Yesterday! As they walked along the edge of the pool, nostalgia stirred with a depth of feeling that astonished her. Was it only yesterday that she had talked to Blake on that lawn-covered terrace beside the pool?

'Penny for them,' Peter asked, 'or are you going to say they aren't worth it?'

'I wasn't going to say any such thing.' She shook her head. 'You shouldn't jump the gun, Peter. I was merely thinking that memories are made of nights like this.'

'And this?' Peter's firm lips brushed her cheeks.

The kiss stopped Lauren in her tracks, causing her mind to become a hotch-potch of thoughts and emotions. The champagne was having a benevolent effect on both of them, she reflected. Even so, she resisted Peter's embrace, and moved ahead of him. Undeterred, he caught up with her. He kissed her again, but this time it was a long, lingering kiss that bespoke awakening passion.

Lauren turned her head sharply. A kiss was a kiss— involvement was something else again. Quickly disengaging herself from Peter's embrace, she gazed ahead and stared straight into the impassive face of Blake Elliott.

Blake spoke evenly. 'Good evening, Miss Fletcher.' There was a look in his eyes which she could not read.

'Good evening, Mr Elliott.' Reaction from the warmth of Peter's embrace, and the chill of this sudden encounter, made her shiver. The movement did not go unnoticed.

'I suggest you go indoors, Miss Fletcher.' Blake made his suggestion sound like an order. Grimly he confronted Peter. 'As for you, Corbett, haven't you more sense than keep Miss Fletcher out here wearing only a thin dress? You know how rapidly the temperature drops.'

The drilling superintendent wasn't joking. Judging by the atmosphere, Lauren would bet that the thermometer had fallen to zero!

Peter flushed with vexation. His lips tightened in a mutinous line. 'Why don't you get off my back, Blake?' he said unexpectedly. 'I know you're my superior, but I'm entitled to a private life.' He laughed bitterly. 'Or have *you* decided that I'm not entitled to that any more?'

Blake's voice was deceptively soft. 'As your superior, I intend to ignore that remark. As man to man, don't you think it's about time you grew up?'

Bewildered by the turn of events, Lauren stood watching Blake. She could see every feature betrayed by the vivid moonlight. The cheek of the man—talking to Peter like that! Could anyone be so hateful? Rallying to Peter's defence, she spoke quickly, her voice precise and icy with anger. 'I'm not on duty now, Mr Elliott. I can please myself whether I freeze to death—I just might prefer the moonlight.' She glared at him. 'What I do out of office hours is no concern of yours.'

'In that you're wrong, Miss Fletcher. Make no mistake about that.' Blake gave her a cold, quelling glance that shrivelled any warmth she had felt for him. 'I don't like members of my staff making a spectacle of themselves in public,' he told her. 'Particularly in an Arab community where strict moral codes are observed—as Corbett should well know.' He said with icy finality, 'If you wish to indulge in romantic behaviour, I suggest you choose a more isolated location. Goodnight.'

With a curt nod, Blake swung on his heels and left them.

'Of all the men,' Lauren raged. 'He's contemptible.'

With an effort at self-control, she touched Peter's arm. 'This is a very public place,' she consoled, 'and not everyone has had the benefit of those super cocktails. What about that meal?'

Peter smiled half-heartedly. 'Yes, okay. Feed the brute in me, then I'll lie at your feet as gentle as a lamb.' His lips quirked upwards. 'I don't want to be led to the slaughter, mind you.'

'Oh, Peter, you're a clown. Bless you.' Lauren's laughter released the tension, and arm-in-arm, they walked cheerfully towards the dining room.

Peter perused the menu. 'What would you like, honey?'

'Melon, I think, then the Chicken in white wine appeals.'

'Good choice. I'll join you and let's have more champagne. Anything less would spoil the cocktails.'

'Such extravagance,' Lauren protested.

Ignoring her protestations, Peter beckoned the wine waiter and ordered a bottle of Bollinger.

'Is it your birthday, Peter?' she asked, remembering it was a celebration.

'Not guilty.'

'How old are you?' Lauren studied him casually, but was unable to determine his age.

Peter chuckled. 'That's what I like about women! They ask outright about age, yet a man hasn't even to hint at such a thing or he's for the high jump.'

'I don't mind you knowing my age. I'm twenty-four—and a bit. How old are you?'

'Persistent, aren't you?' He made a mock-rueful face. 'I'm twenty-seven. Satisfied?'

'No. I want to know a lot more.'

'I'm flattered, but never mind about age and such things. I'm in the mood for soft lights, music and a pretty girl.' He studied her intently. 'You're looking stunning tonight, Lauren.'

'I bet you say that to all the girls,' she teased.

Peter shrugged. 'I don't deny it,' he said, without taking his eyes from her face. 'But you're different. I mean what I say to you.' He looked puzzled as if his statement had been some sort of self-revelation. 'I do mean what I say,' he insisted. 'You've got a quality that's difficult to pinpoint.' He grinned irrepressibly. 'Mmm! Aunt Madeleine would have approved of you.'

Lauren asked, surprised, 'What's Aunt Madeleine got to do with it?'

Peter leaned forward and touched her arm. 'She, my sweet, is the reason for our celebration.' He smiled, yet sadness flickered in his eyes. 'I was her favourite nephew. I heard this morning she'd left me a handsome legacy.' He smiled engagingly. 'Not enough to retire on, mind you, but enough to add zest to living.' He sighed pleasurably. 'Money gives you a wonderful feeling, Lauren. It adds a new dimension to one's life.'

'What was she like?' Lauren asked.

'Delightful,' Peter smiled at his thoughts. 'She was Mother's eldest sister.' He sighed. 'Now Madeleine isn't there, it won't be the same going to Guildford.'

'Guildford, did you say? Isn't that where Blake's father lives?' The instant Lauren spoke, she knew she had spoken thoughtlessly.

'Yes.' His tone was non-committal.

'Peter,' Lauren probed cautiously, 'why are you and Blake continually at loggerheads? You can't meet without sparks flying.' She begged persuasively, 'Won't you tell me, please?'

Peter said abruptly, 'Don't let's talk about it. I've known Blake for some years. It's a long story—and I don't want the memory of it to mar this pleasurable evening.' He frowned. 'Talk of the devil!' he muttered angrily.

Lauren turned round and followed his gaze. With a sense of dismay, she watched Blake and Adele enter the dining room and take a seat where it was impossible for her not to see them.

Peter shrugged. 'Seems we can't get away from the damned man, Lauren. However, he'll be too busy with Adele to bother us.' He gave the nursing Sister a searching look. 'Doesn't she look marvellous, Lauren? That gown she's wearing is superb.' He shrugged expressively. 'Must have been shopping in Beirut—or had it flown in.'

'She should have chosen modelling instead of nursing,' Lauren retorted sharply, seeing all too well why men admired Adele. Unwillingly, she scrutinised the other woman. Her gown was an extravagant creation of flamingo pink, yet she moved in it with ease. Lauren grimaced as she saw Adele look up at Blake—and Blake bend his head forward as if he didn't want to miss one word from those desirable lips. She studied him with determined detachment. He was now dressed in a perfectly tailored lightweight suit. His blue shirt looked expensive and his tie was of maroon silk. She restrained the urge to stare at him and his companion, and kept her gaze firmly on Peter as he perused the menu.

'Sweet?' he asked.

'You've shown me how the rich live—you decide.'

'Okay, honey. I can never resist Peach Melba, so we'll order that.'

Over coffee, he asked earnestly, 'Have you ever been in love, Lauren?'

'Yes,' Lauren replied tonelessly, 'but I got caught up in the race of broken hearts.'

'You, too!' Peter's voice was pensive and he stared moodily in the direction of Adele and Blake.

'Was she lovely, Peter?' Lauren prompted, wondering if he really did care for Adele.

'Fair of face and as pure as the lily,' he said, and Lauren wondered if he jested, but then a shadow crossed his face and made him look sad and wise and haunted.

'What happened, Peter?' she asked gently.

Peter eyed her gravely. 'I told you earlier that you're different, Lauren. She was, too. I'd never met anyone like her.' He shrugged helplessly. 'The trouble was I didn't find out how much she mattered to me until it was too late.'

'Is it too late?' Lauren asked sympathetically.

'Yes.' His eyes darkened at the admission, then he said with a touch of his old flippancy. 'Like a star in the sky, she's out of reach.' His face hardened. 'The truth was I'd had my eyes too long on the ground to recognise the sky when I saw it. Honey and I just weren't in the same orbit— that was the size of it.' He looked across at Lauren and smiled ruefully. 'I don't want to make a second mistake, Lauren,' he said, taking her hand, and giving it a little squeeze. 'You're real.'

'Thanks for a superb evening, Peter,' Lauren said later as

they stood on the verandah of the bungalow. 'Would you like to come in for a drink? Coffee, perhaps?'

'No, thanks, sweetie. I've got an early start.' He moved nearer and took up her hands and kissed the tips of her fingers. 'Next time, we'll really go to town.' He pulled her close and tilted her chin and the next moment his lips were on hers.

As if the touch of Lauren's lips sparked off passion, Peter held her tightly, and she could feel his fingers pressing urgently into her shoulders. She moved restlessly and half turned her head away from Peter's seeking lips, but he was not easily dissuaded. With a stifled exclamation, he pulled her closer, one hand twining her hair, the other caressing the smooth column of her throat; his hand then moved slowly downwards towards the low v-line of her dress.

'You're so lovely, Lauren,' he said huskily. 'Say I stand a chance.'

Firmly Lauren pushed him away. It had been a night of mixed-up emotions. They had drunk champagne and the evening would be one threaded into the fabric of memory, but she wanted no declarations of love—not tonight.

Peter whispered hoarsely, 'I meant what I said. I've always liked the company of beautiful women, but you're different. Say you believe me?' he pleaded.

With gentle fingers, Lauren touched his lips. 'Don't say any more, Peter. Let's get to know each other a lot better than we do now. I like you, but love—well, that's something else again.' She stood on tiptoe and kissed him on the cheek. 'Goodnight, Peter.' She smiled up at him. 'And you know, they were the best cocktails I've ever tasted.'

With a trace of his old charm, he pressed his lips to the palm of her hand. 'If that's the way you want it, princess, I'll play the waiting game. But I intend to make you see things my way—be warned! I'll phone,' he promised. 'Goodnight, honey.' Whistling a pop tune, he walked jauntily to the car.

Lauren stood bemused, and listened to the sound of the

car fade into the night. The garden which had seemed so familiar earlier in the day now seemed a fearful mysterious place, as if, after dark, the desert claimed its own.

Slowly she walked indoors. A curious feeling pervaded her as if she were caught up between happiness and despair. She tried to analyse her emotions and suddenly she longed for home and the comforting presence of her grandparents. The emptiness of the lounge only served to make her loneliness more intense.

Trailing half-heartedly into the kitchen, she switched on the light, then stood waiting for Wally to scuttle under the refrigerator. Wally was a small brown lizard who had made the kitchen his domain. When the house became quiet he would emerge from his hiding place, stretch lazily on the tiled floor or climb the door and cross and re-cross the ceiling. Now Lauren had grown accustomed to the small creature, she stood in the doorway watching him with amusement.

With a sigh of relief she kicked off her high-heeled shoes and wriggled her toes, glad to patter about in her stockinged feet. Making cocoa, she reflected that it had been an eventful day.

Tomorrow, Blake would sit in Mr Stewart's chair.

It was going to be an interesting week.

With that sober thought, Lauren finished her hot drink and went to bed.

Next morning the brightness of the day was deceptive. A cold easterly wind hurried round corners to meet Lauren and she arrived at the office feeling chilled and out-of-tune with herself.

The light flicked on her intercom. 'Bring in your notebook, Miss Fletcher, please,' Blake said tonelessly.

It was strange seeing him sitting in the director's chair, Lauren reflected. She had met his eyes unwaveringly—his gaze was as expressionless as his voice as he told her to be seated.

Blake dictated so rapidly that Lauren's pencil skimmed

over the pages. She was glad the technical phraseology now held no terrors for her, because it was plain to see Blake would prove a hard taskmaster if this morning's work was anything to go by.

As he finished dictating, he handed her a sheaf of papers. 'That lot should keep you out of mischief,' he said, and Lauren fancied the dark eyes betrayed a glimmer of amusement.

She felt a sudden urge to say *unfortunately*, but controlled the impulse and said instead, 'Why has Mr Stewart gone to England?'

'A matter of policy,' was the laconic reply. Blake's hand rested on the telephone, and Lauren knew she was dismissed.

Half an hour later the buzzer summoned her to the director's office. Entering, she saw the general manager seated next to Blake.

'Good morning, sir,' she said.

'My report on Rig Five, Miss Fletcher, please?' Blake's request was curt, but civil.

'Yes, sir,' Lauren replied briskly, and returned to her office. Her mind was ticking over like a computer. She knew she hadn't handled the report, much less filed it. She checked the filing cabinets, but all to no avail. She bit her lip. Where could it be?

Again the buzzer summoned her. 'That report, Miss Fletcher,' Blake frowned impatiently. 'We're waiting.'

'I can't find it in the files, Mr Elliott,' she told him. Conscious of the general manager's presence, she moistened her lips. 'Could it be in Mr Stewart's desk?' she suggested hopefully.

'No, it could not. I've checked,' Blake said sharply. 'I suggest you re-check your filing system, Miss Fletcher.' From the tone of his voice, it was no suggestion—it was a command.

Abashed by the cool dark eyes and the unsmiling mouth, Lauren left the room in despair. Mentally she retraced her every step since her first working day. The report must be important. She heaved a sigh. Where was the wretched folder?

Eventually it transpired that the financial director had taken the report and, with a sigh of relief, Lauren handed the offending document to Blake.

Dismissing her with curt thanks, he turned to the general manager and discussion commenced.

Fuming inwardly, Lauren left the office, her lips clamped firmly together so she could contain the mixture of anger, frustration and heartache that threatened to erupt. She seethed. It *would* have to happen when the drilling superintendent was in command! It was going to seem a long two weeks before kindly Mr Stewart returned.

She had just finished transcribing her earlier notes, and the physical effort required had drained away most of her anger. She was checking the last page when Blake again summoned her to the inner sanctum. He nodded curtly, indicating that she wait. Lauren stood watching him make pencilled notes in the margin of Rig Five report. Hands could tell you a lot about a person, she reflected, and remembered her thoughts at the pool when Blake had placed a hand over hers. A strong hand, that could be gentle. Strong, capable hands that could sign a document quickly, or direct operations at a well-head with speed and direction so a man's life could be saved.

Blake snapped the folder shut, and his action startled her out of her thoughts back to reality. She looked up sharply and concluded that his gaze would be enough to quell a riot, and once more the blood raced rapidly in her veins.

'File that correctly,' he ordered, and threw the contentious folder across the desk. 'Looking in the wrong place can waste valuable time,' he remarked, his voice razor-edged.

'You should know,' Lauren retorted angrily. 'Have you found the missing drilling collar from Rig Three?' Throwing caution to the winds, she raced on, 'Oh, yes, I know just a little about your job, as you know just a little about mine.'

She stopped abruptly, the pounding at her temples matching the rapid beating of her heart. Realising how outspoken she had been, she glanced at Blake, shamefaced, and wondered uneasily if he expected an apology.

Unexpectedly, Blake gave a sudden laugh. 'My favourite aunt warned me about redheads. Red for danger and red for beauty, she used to say.' His eyebrows rose derisively. 'Now I know what she means.' He leaned back in his chair and nodded judicially. 'You deserve dinner on me.'

'I'll hold you to that,' Lauren replied, still trembling, quite unable to believe the transformation. 'My hair is auburn, not red,' she told him, as if that piece of information would explain everything. When Blake didn't comment, she picked up the folder and said, 'Is there anything else, Mr Elliott?'

'No, thanks. At least, not officially.' Blake's eyes narrowed. 'There's one thing I would like to mention.' He eyed her thoughtfully. 'I wouldn't take everything Mr Corbett says to you too seriously.'

The disapproval in his voice re-stoked the flames of Lauren's indignation.

'I'm well able to lead my own life, Mr Elliott,' she retorted resentfully. 'My job is to give satisfaction in the office.' She shrugged defiantly. 'Whether I choose to believe what any man tells me in my private life is my own affair.'

Blake eyed her appraisingly. 'Women are so often attracted to the wrong man. I don't want that to happen to you.'

'And who are you to say who's the right or wrong man for me? I don't know why you dislike Mr Corbett, but since I arrived, Peter's been extremely helpful.'

Blake put a cigarette to his lips, the flame from the lighter illuminating the scorn shadowing his face. 'Mr Corbett is a past master at being helpful to the ladies. I was trying to stop you from getting hurt. Forget it.' His lips twisted cynically. 'You obviously know how to take care of yourself.'

'Yes,' said Lauren, trying to still the tremors that were threatening to knock her off her feet. 'I've had to learn the hard way.' With a proud tilt of her head, she went on, 'I enjoyed dining with Mr Corbett last night. I only hope you enjoyed your evening with Miss Harding.' The inflection in her voice changed to a sliver of steel. 'She certainly gave you her undivided attention!'

Blake's eyes darkened with anger, then his self-control imposed itself and his features hardened into an expressionless mask. 'You've made your point adequately, Miss Fletcher,' he said harshly. 'The subject is closed. Goodnight.' With slow deliberation, he rose to his feet and, ignoring the girl who stood before him, turned to gaze out at the oil town.

Humiliated by Blake's dismissal, Lauren walked out of the office wishing she had told the drilling superintendent exactly what she thought of him and his attitude. The arrogance of the man! His interference made her bristle. How dared he! She vowed she would make up her own mind about her friends. Belatedly she recalled her unfortunate remark about the missing drilling collar; that, and the recent scene, only served to make her feel more apprehensive of the days that lay ahead.

Two hours later she felt more tired than apprehensive, as if the events of the previous evening, together with the physical and emotional fatigue of the day, had taken their toll. With an effort she concentrated on Kath's chatter about Bonfire Night.

'The company put on a super display at the old ridge, Lauren. The world and his wife turns out.'

'Guy Fawkes' Night in the desert is something I find difficult to visualise,' Lauren remarked, aware that some comment was expected. 'It sounds an occasion.'

'It is,' Kath enthused. 'Everything bar the kitchen sink goes on that stack.' She sat silent for a moment and then said sympathetically. 'It's a pity that Peter's been roped in to help with the display, but you'll enjoy yourself with

Molly and her family.' She looked at her friend anxiously. 'You will, won't you?'

'Of course,' Lauren answered with a cheeriness she was far from feeling. She hadn't told Kath about the chill encounter with Blake, or her nagging doubt that the antagonism between Blake and Peter was due to something more deep-rooted than mutual dislike. Lauren didn't want to spoil Kath's pleasure by telling her that she didn't feel crowds were exactly her scene—instead, she smiled and said, 'I'm glad you're going with Ted.'

Kath grinned sheepishly, 'So am I.' She sighed wistfully. 'I rather go for the good doctor,' she said dreamily.

'So I've noticed,' Lauren commented. 'Whenever you talk about that particular medic, your face acquires a rosy glow.'

Kath rose swiftly to her feet. 'Come on, Lauren,' she chivvied. 'Let's get ready. If we chat much longer, we'll miss the floor-show.'

The road to the ridge was heavy with traffic. The oil town was far away from Great Britain, but the procession towards the bonfire seemed to bring a breath of home to the foreign environment in which they lived.

The bonfire stood about thirty feet high. The area had been roped off and to the left of the stack, rope also cordoned off the display set pieces. A fire tender was standing close by and a first-aid post had been erected.

By seven o'clock a large crowd had gathered.

The twins kept chanting, 'Remember, remember the Fifth of November,' and pointing to the line of guys that was waiting to be judged.

Moira said proudly, 'Isn't our guy lovely?' and her hand stole into Lauren's.

'I bet ours is the best,' declared Sharon.

'It's almost a shame to burn him,' Molly said with feeling. 'And, all that sewing, too.'

'Let's hope he wins.' Lauren smiled at the little group. 'I'll keep my fingers crossed,' she promised.

At last the guys were judged and, to the twins' delight, their entry was declared the winner.

'I told you ours was best,' Sharon boasted, and danced with joy as the winning guy was thrown on top of the bonfire. The other entries were carefully placed around the circumference of the stack, and with due ceremony the bonfire was fired.

Soon the greedy flames licked the wood and, gaining sustenance, began to roar with ever-increasing fury as if in competition with the noise of the fireworks now being let off. Lauren smiled at the thought of the immaculate Peter Corbett doing bonfire duty.

Lauren was laughing when a very familiar voice cut in, 'Hello, folks. Can anyone join the fun?'

'Sure,' Alan answered, 'the party's free.'

'Why, of course, Blake,' Molly said happily. 'We're having a lovely time, aren't we, Lauren?'

'Fabulous,' Lauren replied, and despised herself for feeling her heart lift at Blake's appearance.

Blake smiled down at Molly. 'What about letting me spoil you and Lauren for a change? I suggest we go up to the club for dinner after the twins are settled for the night. Be my guests.' He chuckled, and Lauren delighted in the masculine sound. 'Shall we take a vote on it?'

'No need to vote. Grand idea,' Molly declared and Alan confirmed.

Lauren smiled, and this time the reluctance had vanished. 'An offer not to be turned down.'

'Fine,' said Blake, and his answering smile warmed her. 'Now, let's see to the twins.'

As the happy group enjoyed their drinks, the evening breeze was filled with a mixture of saltpetre, sulphur, hot dogs and hamburgers. The aroma was so man-made, Lauren found it difficult to realise that civilisation ended at the fringe of the crowd.

The moon came out of cloud, casting shadows on Blake's face which was a pale silhouette in the flame-filled night.

'Lauren.' His voice sounded husky, unfamiliar. 'It's been quite a day. Wouldn't you say?'

'It certainly has,' she agreed, and wondered if it was a trick of the light that his profile seemed etched with some undefinable emotion. She stood silent. Blake placed an arm around her shoulder and it seemed they shared an understanding of the night. Longing stirred. The enchantment of the saffron land was binding them together yet again.

'Blake.' Alan's voice broke the spell. 'We'd better tidy up, and return the empties.'

'Okay, Alan.' Blake smiled at Lauren. 'Later,' he said.

As the men moved away, Lauren saw Sharon running towards the bonfire. With ease, the child scrambled underneath the rope that cordoned off the stack. 'Sharon!' she yelled, and was galvanised into action. With fear speeding her steps, she ran towards the enclosure. Vaguely she thought she heard Blake shout, but the crackle of flames and her concern for Sharon made her pay no heed. Speeding ahead of Sharon, she grabbed hold of the little girl and pulled her sharply from the stack, wincing as the heat from the fire scorched her skin.

Sharon resisted. 'No! Let me go! I want to see if the guy has been all burned away.'

'No, Sharon,' Lauren said severely. 'Go to Mummy.'

With that command she pushed the child towards Molly. A swishing noise filled her ears and her gaze became transfixed as she watched a rocket misfire. Mesmerised by its movement, Lauren could only stare at it, filled with the terrible inevitability that it was speeding towards her. Pain seared the side of her head. As she fell, her one instinct was to call for Blake to come to her aid. Faces, shadowed and strange in the firelight, confused her. There was a surging movement around her, then Blake's dark figure was there, and instinctively Lauren stretched out her arms.

Effortlessly Blake picked up the slender girl, and cradling her like a child, made his way through the crowd that was being drawn to the spot like a magnet.

Lauren was aware only of sensations following one upon the other with electrifying speed. She could hear Blake's heart beat with an insistent hammering that seemed to throb through his very jacket. There was warmth in the feel of him. She clung to him, feeling comfort and security in the circle of the strong arms.

In desperate endeavour she tried to focus, but the pain in her head grew more intense, crushing all speech, even thought, then oblivion claimed her, holding her its prisoner.

CHAPTER SIX

LAUREN lay in a world of silence and shadow, yet it did not bother her that she could not move. Her head was full of little stabbing pains that darted in and out of her thoughts as she tried to think where she was.

She opened her eyes, only to shut them quickly as the sharp sunlight blurred her vision with its golden blaze. She could smell antiseptic and her head felt swathed in clouds of cotton wool. Tentatively, she again opened her eyes, focussed, and became aware of a young nurse standing by her bed, which only confused her more. She tried to speak, but failed. She struggled to sit up, only to find compelling hands easing her back against the pillows.

'Lie still,' a soothing voice insisted. 'Don't try to talk.'

Lauren moistened her lips.

'A drink?' The nurse nodded in comprehension. 'Yes, I understand.' Within moments she returned, and holding the drinking cup with expert hands said gently, 'Little sips, at first.'

The water washed over Lauren's parched lips, its healing flow stilling the clamouring of her throat, arid as any desert waste.

'Ah! That is better, so?'

'How long have I been here? Please tell me,' Lauren pleaded.

'Since last night.' The nurse turned at the sound of the door opening. 'Here comes Sister Harding,' she said softly.

Lauren stared at the woman approaching the bed, suddenly recognising the stranger in crisp white uniform as the elegant Adele.

'How are you feeling, Miss Fletcher?' Adele asked, feeling Lauren's pulse and looking at the fob-watch pinned on to her dress.

'Hazy,' Lauren replied. 'What happened?'

'One of the rockets shot off at the wrong angle and caught the side of your head. It could have been worse—you've only had to have a few stitches.' The smile she gave Lauren was cool, professional. 'You've had a lucky escape, so don't complain about the size of your headache. Now you must rest,' she told her patient, 'otherwise I won't allow visitors.'

Lauren touched the unfamiliar thickness enveloping her head. 'Adele,' she said with agitation, 'don't tell me not to talk. These bandages?'

'Don't worry, they'll be replaced by a plaster. We've had to cut your hair, but it will soon grow again.' Adele's voice was insistent. 'I've told Mr Elliott he can visit you this afternoon. He's always so considerate of his staff.' The smile she gave Lauren didn't reach her eyes, then softly as a shadow, Adele moved away.

At the thought of Blake's impending visit, Lauren waited in a mood of restless excitement. However hard she tried to remind herself that Adele was the woman who attracted the drilling superintendent, the memory of Blake holding her persisted, threatening to trigger off a multitude of emotions. Finally she slept.

Aroused by the sudden sound of voices, sleep-dazed, she glanced up and saw Adele, closely followed by Blake.

'I've brought Mr Elliott to see you,' Adele told her, and with solicitude straightened the pillows. 'I've told him not to stay too long.' She turned to Blake. 'I'll see you later,' she said, and left the ward.

'Hello, Lauren,' Blake said softly. 'Feeling rough?'

'A bit.'

'How does it feel to be a heroine?'

'Heroine?' Lauren bit her lip in concentration. 'Yes, now I understand. Is Sharon all right?'

'Fine, apart from being blistered by her mother's tongue.

Molly and Alan are so grateful. They don't know how to thank you. If you hadn't grabbed Sharon...!'

Lauren looked embarrassed. 'I'm glad she's unhurt.'

Weakness made her want to weep, yet it was not weakness alone that made her feel so helpless. Seeing Blake so near to her, she felt a desperate urgency to touch him, to talk to him. Instead, she spoke Adele's name, and wondered why she should mention her rival. 'Adele tells me I've just missed being scalped. She said one of the rockets misfired and nosedived in my direction.'

'Even rockets know where the attraction lies!' Blake said tenderly.

'I'm glad you got to me in time. Thanks.'

'Think nothing of it.' He shrugged expressively. 'Seriously, how are you feeling?' he asked gently, and covered her hand with his own.

Lauren trembled at his touch. 'Apart from a splitting headache, fine,' she answered shakily. 'Perhaps it won't be too long before I'm back on the job,' she said anxiously.

'Work is the last thing you've got to worry about,' he told her. 'The main concern is to get back on your feet. As for work, we'll cope.' He grinned. 'Did no one ever tell you that once released, the oil just gives itself up?' The pressure of his hand increased. 'I'd better go before I'm thrown out. Adele said I hadn't to stay too long, and she's a tartar for discipline.' His mouth softened. 'I'll come again soon.'

Lauren tried to rest, but relentlessly her thoughts kept returning to Blake. She lay there puzzling over the many facets of the man who was assuming such importance in her life. He was also important in Adele's life. And Blake himself—the man of authority and mysticism—how deeply did he care? With that thought, Lauren slipped into uneasy slumber.

When Lauren awoke the room was dim. She felt hot and clammy and was glad when the nurse sponged her. She had just finished a light meal when Adele came into the ward.

Straightening the bedcovers, Adele said silkily, 'I'm not

allowing visitors tonight. Your temperature has risen—no doubt due to the excitement this afternoon.' She smiled without sincerity. 'People have phoned and some gifts have arrived.'

As Lauren fingered the softness of a delicate green bed-jacket and touched the tablets of soap, and the cologne; a lump in her throat heralded tears at the kindness of her new friends. 'How good people are,' she whispered.

'And look at these!' Adele held a superb bouquet fastened with a bow of blue satin for Lauren to admire. The girl gazed in wonder at the gladioli, carnations and irises, their colours jewel-bright against a background of fern.

Avidly Lauren stared at them, realising how hungry she was for the sight of such natural colour after even a few short weeks in this tawny, sun-scorched land. 'I don't understand,' she stammered. 'One can't get flowers like these, here?'

'No,' Adele answered. 'These have obviously been flown in from Beirut.'

Lauren shook her head in bewilderment. 'They're gorgeous,' she said breathlessly. 'Do tell me who sent them.'

Adele took the card from the envelope and as she scanned the message, Lauren saw her stiffen. 'The flowers are from Mr Elliott,' Adele said curtly, and abruptly handed Lauren the card. 'I must say Mr Elliott has gone to a lot of trouble for a member of his staff,' she commented, raising delicate eyebrows, 'but then he's a kind man, don't you agree?'

'Of course,' Lauren replied.

'I must tell him how pleased you are with the bouquet when we dine later.' Adele's voice dropped to a confidential whisper. 'Tonight is a special occasion—we're going to discuss future plans.' She laughed coyly. 'No prizes for guessing what that means—but I suppose the traditional crossword clue would read "has associations with orange-blossom".' She bent forward to pick up the flowers and Lauren could have sworn malice gleamed in the amber eyes, but when she stood up Adele's face was without guile. She smiled and Lauren had a momentary impression of spiteful satisfaction.

A few days later Lauren returned to the office. Blake told her to take it easy, but paperwork soon builds up, and in next to no time Lauren felt she had never been away. And so November progressed into December. Mr Stewart had been delayed, and it seemed unlikely that the director would return to Akhmar before the New Year.

One morning a week before Christmas Blake sauntered towards her desk. 'How's the Arabic?' he asked amiably.

'*Mashallah*,' Lauren replied proudly. 'That does mean wonderful, doesn't it?'

Blake's dark eyebrows rose a fraction. 'The literal translation is *what wonders God hath willed*—but don't worry,' he said dryly, 'you're improving.'

She saw his alert eyes take in the invitation card on her desk. 'I see you've been invited to the general manager's cocktail party?'

'Yes,' she answered, then said hesitantly, 'I understand it's a politely worded command.'

Blake nodded. 'You could say that. Every year the general manager and his good lady invite local dignitaries and certain staff members to a Christmas gathering.' He leaned forward and Lauren willy-nilly felt her heart surge as she felt his breath warm upon her face. 'Here's your chance to meet a real live Sheikh,' he joked. 'Isn't that what all young girls dream about?'

'But of course,' Lauren replied, sugar-sweet, determined not to let Blake see how easily he could upset her equilibrium.

Their laughter was interrupted by the ringing of the red telephone.

Blake grabbed the receiver. As he spoke, Lauren could see his eyebrows knit together, a frown darkening the autocratic face. With a muttered oath he replaced the receiver.

'I'm off to Rig Five,' he told her. 'We've got to core-barrel for a quarter of a mile,' he said tersely, then he was gone.

It was late afternoon when he returned, hot and dusty, yelling for black coffee. 'Join me,' he told Lauren, then lit a cigarette, and slid wearily into his chair.

The coffee seemed to refresh him. Afterwards, he pushed aside the empty cup and eyed Lauren speculatively. 'So you want to know more about core-barrelling? In brief, it's taking samples for the geologists. They usually require one or two samples from each well, drilled at varying depths. Routine stuff, no problem. Now, they want the next quarter of a mile core-barrelled!' He shrugged with exasperation. 'The major problem is time. The drilling crews have to pull out three-quarters of a mile of pipe, fit the barrel, re-run the pipe and continue *that* process every thirty feet.' He snorted. 'We can well do without that delay at this stage. I estimate another six weeks will be needed to complete that job.'

'I'd like to go out to a rig some time to see for myself,' Lauren said. 'Would that be possible?'

'A drilling rig isn't exactly the right location for a woman,' Blake said brusquely. He shrugged and pushed a hand through hair which was plastered with sand and sweat. 'Hell! I need a cool shower, a change of clothing, not to mention iced lager on tap. I'm off now. Be ready at six o'clock and I'll escort you personally to that cocktail party.' There was a gleam in his eyes as he whispered, 'I must see that you're introduced to all the right people.'

'Thanks, Blake,' Lauren said meekly, ignoring his teasing. 'I'll be ready.'

As she lazed in a bath of scented foam, she let her thoughts drift. Tonight she would wear her dress of jade-green silk. This was the first time Blake had arranged to escort her, and she wanted the evening to be special. She tried to puzzle out why he wasn't escorting Adele. Surely she would be there? The thought nagged at her as she dressed, but was dispelled as she gazed into the mirror and saw herself arrayed in all her jade-green glory. She felt beautiful—she looked beautiful, she assured herself.

Blake was dressed in an impeccably tailored suit of charcoal-grey and his blue shirt highlighted the colour of his eyes. Lauren studied him and thought how attractive he looked, and her heart turned over with longing as he greeted her. 'You look enchanting, Lauren,' he complimented. 'I don't know why, but you remind me of a sea-nymph.' His hand touched her shorn hair. 'Perhaps that hair-cut they gave you at the hospital has something to do with it.'

The driveway of the general manager's residence was already crowded with cars. A huge Christmas tree, festive with lights, dominated the entrance and lanterns and holly decorated the rooms.

After greeting their host, Blake led the way to a quiet corner and disappeared to find her a drink.

Fascinated, she watched him move through the crowd. The jewelled colours of the ladies' gowns were highlighted by the formal suits of the men. The flowing robes of the Arabs emphasised the meeting of East and West.

She caught a glimpse of Peter at the far end of the room. The very embodiment of the well-educated handsome Englishman, it wasn't difficult to understand his attraction for the opposite sex. A smile brightened his face when he saw Lauren, and it was with a sense of relief that she saw his attention captured by an Arab official.

She felt guilty at her sense of relief—or was it apprehension? She knew only too well how the atmosphere could become instantly charged with animosity when Blake and Peter met, and she didn't want anyone to spoil tonight.

Lauren saw Blake, followed by a waiter, carrying their drinks, then her heart sank as she noticed Adele at his side. Wearing an oyster-silk creation, its simplicity shrieking Paris, Adele looked fabulous.

'I thought you couldn't make it tonight, Adele?' Blake remarked, but didn't seem upset that she hadn't bothered to inform him otherwise, and this fact puzzled Lauren.

'I forgot to tell you they changed the duty rota,' she said in that seductive tone she used when speaking to men. 'Forgive me.' As if noticing Lauren for the first time, she greeted the girl coolly. 'I hope you're now fully recovered, Lauren?'

'Quite recovered, Adele,' Lauren replied evenly.

'It's kind of Blake to escort you to your first major cocktail party, Lauren,' and there was a purring note in her voice that Lauren distrusted. 'I think you look a little tired,' Adele went on, with hypocritical concern. 'Perhaps you should leave the party early. We don't want you to be in hospital again.'

'Never mind about the professional opinion, Adele. Lauren looks beautiful,' Blake said easily. 'Talking about the medical profession,' he continued, 'I see the Chief Medical Officer is beckoning you to join him.'

Adele flashed Lauren a look of malice, then said pointedly, 'I'll see you later, Blake.' There was no mistaking her message ... she meant alone.

Blake gave no indication that he intended meeting Adele, but propelled Lauren towards the centre of the large reception room. 'Let's circulate,' he suggested. 'There must be any number of people you've yet to meet.'

They joined a small group and the animated conversation was as heady as wine. Lauren was grateful for the merry chatter—it effectively shut out the memory of the malice she had seen on Adele's face.

'Let's get a breath of fresh air,' Blake suggested and, taking Lauren's arm, he led her towards the French windows.

'Blake Elliott, is it not?'

To Lauren's surprise, an Arab of striking appearance placed a glass of cordial on a small side table, and with arms outstretched, greeted Blake with evident delight.

Blake returned the greeting and clasped the hands of the Arab firmly in his own. 'Hassan,' he said warmly. 'How good it is to see you. I heard you were due back from the States.'

'And how good it is to see you, and your so charming companion.'

Blake introduced the wealthy Arab with genuine warmth.

The Sheikh Ben Abdul Hassan, a member of the ruling family, wore a cream robe edged with gold. His white headdress was bound by a black and gold *agal*. There was a proud lift to his head which made him seem taller than he was, and his eyes were like dark coals glowing in his thin autocratic face, which Lauren saw was now relaxed and smiling.

'Enchanted, *mademoiselle*,' he greeted her. He touched his chest, lips and forehead with his fingers in the gesture of *salaam* that comes so naturally to the Arab. 'How fortunate is my friend Blake to have the company of such a beautiful woman. But then I have always thought him a most fortunate man.'

'There speaks a man of wisdom,' said Blake, and Lauren watched the two men exchange glances of mutual amusement.

'You have recently arrived from England, Miss Fletcher?' enquired the Sheikh.

'Yes,' Lauren told him. 'It's difficult to believe it was only a few weeks ago.'

'Now it is December! You will be glad you are not in England with its inclement weather.' He lifted his shoulders. 'The thought of the London fog and the swirling snow makes me shiver.'

'You know England, then?'

'Ah, yes, *mademoiselle*, I know your country well. Blake and I were at Oxford together, then our paths led us in different directions. I went to America. Blake came to my country.' He nodded sagely. 'Now our paths cross again.' He turned to Blake. 'We spent many happy times at Oxford, did we not, my friend?'

'We did indeed, Hassan,' Blake confirmed.

Lauren listened, fascinated and amazed at their in-depth conversation. She had realised Blake was a well-educated man, his technical knowledge alone could not have been acquired easily, yet listening to him talking to Hassan about their undergraduate days, the various personalities known to both men, she saw yet another aspect of the man who dominated her personal horizon more and more as the days passed.

Hassan's voice was full of charm as he apologised to Lauren. 'I cannot invite you, lovely lady, for this day I speak of is not for the feminine sex.'

Lauren looked helplessly at Blake. She had been so busy thinking about the drilling superintendent, she hadn't heard Hassan's previous remark.

Blake saw her look and realised her attention had wandered. Smiling at Hassan, he said with sincerity, 'I shall look forward to joining your hunting party on Boxing Day. It's some time since I enjoyed the pleasure of a day's sport in the desert.' He looked at Lauren with twinkling eyes. 'As Hassan says, Lauren, no ladies allowed.' He shrugged expressively. 'However, to compensate, I'll take you to visit the old city,' he promised.

Not to be outdone, Hassan spoke, his voice deep, ambiguous. 'I, too, must invite you to some occasion you will remember.'

'I shall look forward to it. Thank you,' Lauren answered formally.

Later, as Hassan bade her goodnight, Lauren could not but be aware of the admiration kindling in the Sheikh's eyes. Suddenly she felt uneasy as if a feather of premonition had brushed her skin.

She settled herself in Blake's car, feeling sorry that the cocktail party was over and the evening lay ahead, apparently empty and unfulfilled, when Blake said unexpectedly,

'I owe you a dinner.'

'So you do!' Lauren exclaimed. She wrinkled her nose. 'I thought you'd never ask.'

'Where shall we dine? The club, or my place?'

'I'm your guest. You choose.'

'Okay. My place it is.' He grinned. 'Suliman's an expert at producing a meal at short notice.'

'That's fine, then.' Lauren wondered suddenly what Adele's reaction would be if she knew about the invitation. Unfavourable—certainly. She also wondered if Blake had remembered Adele's remark that she would see him later, but as they entered Blake's bungalow, the nursing Sister was forgotten.

Fascinated, Lauren gazed around the main room. The air-conditioning unit throbbed life into the empty lounge, the tiled floor of which was strewn with two superb Kashan rugs. In contrast to the teak furniture and comfortable armchairs, a huge sandalwood brass-bound chest and a handsome camel-litter of coloured leather added an Eastern influence to the room which she saw was essentially masculine.

Bookshelves dominated the far wall, and on a small table near a desk lay a glass case which contained a steel drilling bit, similar to the one Lauren had observed in Mr Stewart's office. Remembering the director's comments that it was the bit he had brought his first well in with, she smiled. It would appear that at heart these hard-headed oil men were also sentimental.

Blake pointed to a door. 'While you powder your nose, I'll go and hustle Suliman.'

He smiled and strode from the room, and Lauren headed for the bathroom.

After applying fresh make-up, she stared at her reflection. Like Cinderella, she had been transformed. She could hardly believe that tonight was real. It possessed all the quality of a dream. Yet despite her happiness, she could not rid herself of the feeling that the dream would be broken and she would wake up and find reality. She smiled away the thought and returned to the lounge.

Dinner over, Blake poured liqueurs, then sat beside

TAKE THESE *3 free* Masquerade HISTORICALS

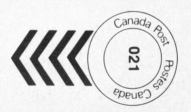

Lauren, chatting, asking her if she had enjoyed the evening.

Lauren nodded and smiled happily.

'Did you like Hassan?' Blake eyed her curiously as if her answer were important to him.

'Yes. A charming man,' Lauren replied steadily, willing away the premonition that persisted at the mention of the Sheikh.

Blake pulled deeply on his cigarette, thought furrowing his brow. 'Hassan lives in a complex world. He's had the education of a Westerner, yet deep inside he clings to the old beliefs. So much his intelligence will accept, so much his mind rejects. He's part of a new generation that stands at the end of one road, and looks to see where the new road leads. The finding of oil, the influence of Western civilisation, the new economic structure of the developing countries, make it impossible for him to remain in the past. He's emerging into a new world, yet within himself, I feel, he finds cause for conflict.'

'Western influence has obviously altered a lot of their ideas. Do they still hold fast to their old traditions?'

'It's not easy to generalise. In the areas where Western civilisation has become established, many of the old customs have all but perished.'

'What about women?' Lauren asked thoughtfully. 'I've often wondered why the Arab woman wears that all-enveloping black cloak.'

Blake smiled. 'In the old days, the Arab tribesmen used to say an uncovered woman was an immoral one, and asked why a wife would want to show herself to anyone but her husband.' He shrugged regretfully. 'Slowly but surely the old traditions are being forgotten, or at least not held in the reverence they were.'

'It's inevitable, I suppose,' Lauren said gravely.

Blake stubbed out his cigarette, then said without preamble, 'Hassan may ask to see you, Lauren. Don't do anything rash ... Out here, even the simplest action can be misconstrued.'

Lauren smiled and shook her head. 'I won't do anything rash, as you put it,' she promised him.

Blake smiled, and once more Lauren wished he wouldn't look at her with such disturbing intensity. If he but knew it, she was defenceless against his charms.

At last Blake spoke, and the magic moment was over. 'Time I took you home.' He stood up and putting his cigarettes in his pocket said as an afterthought, 'Oh, there's a book I thought you might find interesting. It's by Gilbran, the prophet. I've left it out on the desk.' He smiled. 'Pick it up, and I'll start the car while you get it.'

Adjusting to Blake's change of mood, Lauren nodded and walked towards the desk. She stretched out her hand to pick up the book and, as she did so, her other hand inadvertently moved the pages of a letter, and startled, she found herself gazing at the snapshot of a young girl.

Honey-coloured hair fell in natural waves about a piquant face. The large eyes held a sad, almost questioning look. Across the bottom of the photograph a message had been scrawled. 'To Blake, with love. Tracey.'

Lauren drew in a deep breath, annoyed to feel the prick of tears behind her eyelids. The feeling that the night was a fragile world that could be broken at any minute was now a fact. The pieces lay on the floor. Lauren sighed. The ball was over. Midnight had come for Cinderella—the evening had been a dream of little substance. Sadly she picked up the book and walked towards the car.

As Blake drove her homewards, her silence prompted him to ask her if she was tired.

'Yes,' she replied. 'It's been quite a day, one way and another.'

When they reached the bungalow Blake helped her out of the car and guided her towards the gate. She strove to appear composed, but as she turned to say goodnight, she could not suppress a shiver.

Blake put his arms around her shoulders and drew her close. The action made her recall clearly his scorn as he had watched Peter kiss her at the Dolphin Club. The words of Adele telling her about an orange-blossom occasion screamed through her mind, and again she relived the misery she had experienced when finding the photograph of the mysterious Tracey.

In that split second, the fragments merged into a heart-breaking canvas making her recognise the moment of truth. She was in love with Blake Elliott.

As Blake's fingers gripped her shoulders, she deliberately resisted his physical charm that was tearing her body apart.

'Relax,' Blake said gently. 'There's no need to retreat into your shell. I won't harm you. I'm only going to kiss you goodnight.'

Lauren stiffened. 'You're only going to kiss me. Just like that,' she mocked. 'You think because you saw Peter kissing me, I don't mind who does the kissing.' She swallowed painfully, but said in a voice she didn't recognise as her own. 'Well, Mr Elliott, I do. I mind very much.' She laughed scornfully. 'Men are all the same! A girl only has to show a passing interest and men are so damned egotistical, they think she's hooked.' She could hear the mockery in her voice and despised herself for falling in love again. She hadn't learned her lesson well, she reflected wryly. This time the love was for real.

Blake swore softly and his fingers bit even deeper into her flesh. 'Seeing you've mentioned Peter,' he said, 'let me show you how a man kisses.'

His lips, demanding and relentless, sought hers. This was no lover's tender kiss, but one of fire and fury that bruised her and shook her emotions to their foundations. Instinct made her want to fight, but desire leapt to flame. Like Galatea, Lauren was brought to life.

As Blake's arms tightened about her, she was aware of the passion of his embrace. In that bitter-sweet ecstasy of response she felt herself to be swirling into space, where no one else mattered except Blake Elliott and Lauren Fletcher. Then pride reared its head. Enraged with herself for even that small moment of surrender, Lauren put her arms against Blake's chest and strove to push him away, but her strength was no match for his.

In mockery, his arms held her like bands of iron. He smiled sardonically; only his uneven breathing indicating the depth of his passion.

Lauren moved her face, and then quickly looked up at him, surprising a look that held both bewilderment and anger. Wearily she dismissed the expression as a trick of the moonlight.

Wanting to hurt him, even as she had been hurt, she lashed out with verbal fury. 'I was right the first time I saw you,' she said. 'Even though you are the drilling superintendent, you're a roughneck at heart.' Her breath came in quick, uneven gasps. 'I've heard tell you only love your oil rig—well, let that be your mistress. It's the only one you're likely to possess permanently!'

Even in the uneasy shadows of the night, she saw his face become white with controlled rage and for what seemed to be an eternity he stood as if carved from stone, then his pent-up wrath uncoiled, and was immediately controlled. Breathing deeply, with icy deliberation, he pushed her away from him.

'If I'm that undesirable, let's not prolong the agony. At least for future reference, my girl, you'll know what grade to aim for.' The words fell heavily. Lauren felt their impact and their chill.

'You're contemptible!' she snapped, and before she could prevent herself, her fingers came into sharp contact with his cheek.

He caught her wrist in a vice-like grip. 'I wouldn't do that again, if I were you,' he told her, his voice soft and menacing—a stranger's voice.

Lauren said nothing. She felt drained of all emotion, too disillusioned, too shattered, even to feel vulnerable.

Blake stood in silence, and, in some curious way, she hated the silence more than his sarcasm.

Half afraid to move, she turned to leave him, when he once more gripped her shoulders. 'I don't know what's got into you, Lauren,' he said brusquely, 'but I suggest you go back to boys like Corbett—that way you'll be certain that matters won't get out of hand.' He shrugged carelessly. 'Goodnight, sweetheart,' he jeered. 'Pleasant dreams.' Abruptly, he turned on his heel and left her.

Lauren watched him as he walked to the car and flung himself into the driving seat without a backward glance in her direction. Vision blurred, she watched the car disappear from sight, then with slow steps she walked along the concrete path to the solace of her room.

The evening which had held such promise had turned into a nightmare. As the cold winds blew in from the desert, they carried with them the seeds of desolation that found fertile ground in the place Lauren Fletcher called her heart.

CHAPTER SEVEN

SEATED at her desk next morning. Lauren was determined not to let the events of the previous evening cloud the day.

Of Blake there was no sign. Kept busy with insistent enquiries from people anxious to speak to the drilling superintendent personally, Lauren felt irritated by his lack of consideration. How could she be expected to be efficient if he failed to inform her of his whereabouts?

After a particularly irate call from the general manager that Blake be contacted without delay, Lauren seethed with resentment after several telephone calls proved fruitless.

Two hours later a door slammed, someone stumbled against a chair, and she heard Blake's muttered oaths as he entered the office.

With heart pounding, she entered the director's room. Blake was sitting behind the desk, apparently unharmed, but looking disgruntled. Fatigue ridged his skin which now had a greyish tinge and his eyes were red-rimmed as if from lack of sleep.

When he saw Lauren, he said curtly, 'Yes?'

'The general manager wants you to telephone him, at once.'

Blake nodded. 'Okay. Meanwhile, bring me gallons of coffee—black as the ace of spades.'

'Right away, sir.'

As Lauren addressed him formally, Blake's look was quite impassive and she knew then that he had no intention of referring to the episode on the verandah.

Guiltily, she lowered her eyes and went to make the coffee. She knew she had been unpardonably rude to the oil man the previous evening, and her behaviour must have seemed to him puzzling and capricious. Would he ever forgive her for the things she had said?

The thought hammered in her brain and, when she returned with the coffee, her hands trembled so much that some of the liquid spilled into the saucer. In her agitation, she knocked the tray crashing to the floor. Its metallic sound reverberated harshly in the room which was otherwise quiet except for the clicking of the telex machine.

'Do you have to make that racket, Miss Fletcher?'

'Sorry,' Lauren murmured contritely, conscious of Blake's critical gaze as she bent to pick up the tray.

With a weary gesture, he picked up the telephone and she could see his features harden as he spoke to the general manager. 'I've been at Rig Three since four this morning,' he rasped. 'One of my drilling crew had an accident.' His lips tightened. 'Yes! I'll let you have details.'

With emphasis, he replaced the receiver. With a harassed movement he rubbed a hand across his forehead. Lauren could see the tension in the set of the broad shoulders. His lips were a taut line as if will-power would not let him relax.

She wanted to go to him, touch him, but she knew she could not. She had no alternative but to stand aside and remain detached. She said the only thing she could say. 'I'm sorry to hear about the accident,' she faltered. 'Was it very nasty?'

'All accidents are nasty,' Blake declared.

Lauren thought she detected strain in his voice, but his face betrayed no emotion.

From that moment, the office became a battlefield of screaming telephones, urgent telex calls, and insistent callers. By the end of the afternoon, Lauren's resolution to remain calm and impersonal was beginning to flounder. More than once she restrained herself from 'jumping to the bait', and it was with an inward sigh of relief that she watched the drilling superintendent sign the final document.

Handing her the correspondence folder, Blake said with deceptive calm, 'You intrigue me, Lauren.'

'In what way?' she asked defensively.

'You might well ask! Last night for no apparent reason, you blew your top, yet today, when I've been like a bear with a sore head, you've remained completely unruffled.' He smiled disarmingly. 'The perfect secretary—I never thought it would be my good fortune to employ such a paragon of virtue.'

Lauren resisted the urge to quibble and say she was actually employed by the oil company. Instead she smiled coolly. 'As you say, the perfect secretary.' Quelling the rebellion that ached to be released, she continued, 'The answer is simple. Last night was personal. Today I'm on duty.'

'Is that so?' Blake's tone lowered perceptibly, yet his words were sharp with serrated subtlety. 'What you're telling me is that a good secretary knows when to tread softly?'

Lauren nodded, hesitantly, scenting danger as his eyes narrowed.

'Let me tell you that being a good secretary has nothing to do with it,' he rapped out. The flat of his hand slapped the desk-top with such force that she involuntarily stepped backwards, stiffening as she took the verbal blow of his next onslaught. 'You, Lauren,' he said sarcastically, 'are just about as constant as a chameleon!'

His sarcasm seared her, and trying to keep a balanced sense of bad temper, Lauren said evenly, 'I think it's totally unfair of you, Mr Elliott, to use your superior position to make that type of remark during office hours—knowing full well that retaliation on my part could cost me my job.' She managed to retain a calm expression, but inwardly she was bubbling like a witches' brew. 'Let me tell you if ever we do meet outside office hours again—an event which I think highly unlikely after last night's episode—I shan't hesitate to tell you exactly what I think of you.' Her cheeks burned as she held up her head defiantly.

The silence that followed her outburst made her move restlessly. Holding her breath, she waited for Blake's wrath to fall.

Surprisingly, he laughed. 'Excellent, Miss Fletcher,' he said with the air of a man who was laughing at his own thoughts. 'Now I know it's you. I was beginning to think you had a double.'

Lauren watched him suspiciously as he selected a cigarette, lit it, and lay back in his chair, surveying her with tolerant amusement.

'Don't let yourself be converted to the Arab idea that women should be submissive.' The tone of his voice suggested such a conversion would be next to impossible.

Before she could take up the cudgels in her defence, Blake spoke again.

'As a product of Western emancipation, I find you much more exciting, Lauren.'

His face was alive with sardonic delight as he said with evident enjoyment, 'If your social calendar is free, what about coming with me to Quamat next Friday?' He held her gaze. 'Then you'll be able to have the verbal battle of your life—if you dare.'

Taken aback by Blake's invitation, Lauren took long gulps of air to restore her equilibrium. Once again, Blake Elliott had turned the tables on her. She could be churlish and refuse his invitation, but that would be cutting off her nose to spite her face. She wanted to see Quamat and she knew Blake would be the best person to accompany her.

Trying to conceal her thoughts, she replied haughtily, 'Friday will be fine.' But her heart was not deceived and thudded against her ribs as the words of acceptance left her lips. Once more she was made aware that the man facing her could disarm her at a moment's notice. Why, oh, why couldn't she be in love with a pleasant, ordinary man, instead of this ruthless, egotistical, sarcastic brute?

Friday dawned bright and beautiful. As Lauren waited for
Blake to arrive, she experienced the excitement she had
known as a child when going on holiday.

'Hello,' she greeted him. 'There's so much I want to
see.'

'Goodness,' he grinned, 'you *are* excited!'

'Where shall we go first?' she asked joyfully. 'I've got
my shopping list.' She smiled. 'There are so many things I
want to see and do.'

Blake smiled indulgently. 'Settle down, child, or you'll
be too exhausted to take the trip, let alone do Christmas
shopping.'

At his bidding, Lauren settled herself comfortably in the
car. Her heart sang silently with the sheer joy of living. Her
spirits matched the blue-gold morning as sand kissed sky,
and the flame over the gas separator unit feathered the skyline crimson.

As Blake swung on to a desert track, she exclaimed with
apprehension, 'I thought we were going to Quamat?'

'We are.'

'Across the desert?'

'Yes.' He glanced at her mockingly. 'I'm a desert man,
not an admin type. Remember?'

'I'm hardly likely to forget it,' Lauren retorted smilingly.
Blake's remark was a dig at Peter, she told herself, but
whatever quarrel they had, it was their own. This day be-
longed to her.

During that drive from the airport, Peter had driven
along a tarmac road, bordered on either side by stretches of
sand, scorched and solitary. Now, with Blake beside her,
the countryside took on a new dimension. It had been rain-
ing and the land was wrinkled with depressions that contained water. Brilliant green leaves of purple iris and clumps
of clover were scattering the surface of the flat brown earth.

'Isn't it beautiful?' Lauren enthused. 'And changeable,
too.'

Blake gave a low-throated chuckle. 'Now you understand

why men compare the desert with beautiful women—and as many darned moods, too.'

Lauren's gaze was still riveted on the parched land that overnight had changed into a garden. She turned to speak to Blake, experiencing pleasure as she gazed at his firm, proud profile. 'What I can't understand is how anything can blossom in this wasteland. One minute it's devoid of life. The next, you have this miracle. How does it happen?'

'It rains,' Blake said dryly.

'Tell me more?' Lauren gazed in wonder at the landscape which resembled some gigantic patchwork quilt with which Nature had seen fit to clothe her naked wasteland.

Blake turned to give her an easy smile. 'The sand soaks up the moisture and the living cells underneath the ground grow quickly and flower. The heat of the sun gets at them, and just as quickly, they disappear.' He shrugged regretfully. 'It's a rare beauty, rare because it lasts so little time.'

'Will man ever irrigate the desert?'

'Perhaps,' he said, his shrewd blue eyes regarding her gravely. 'Tremendous projects have been put forward for reclamation, but results aren't achieved overnight.'

He turned his attention to the track, and Lauren stared out of the window. Very conscious of his physical nearness, she became aware of her own desires, but firmly she put the lid on her emotional responses and told herself she was out to enjoy a day in Quamat, and that was all.

They had driven some ten miles when they came to an Arab settlement. The dwellings consisted mostly of mud-and-mat *serifas*, although a number of huts were made of mud, flattened petrol drums, and roofed with corrugated steel. A group of women, enshrouded in their black *abbi*, sat on the ground weaving and gossiping. Dusky children played or guarded the livestock. Camels stared disdainfully, their vicious temperaments momentarily hidden, and lean dogs barked their awareness of the presence of strangers.

In startling contrast, modern American cars were parked alongside some of the primitive shacks. Lauren blinked to see if they were a mirage, but when she looked again, the cars were every bit as real as the rest of the encampment.

She shook her head, bemused. She felt that the colour slides depicting two centuries had become mixed up and it was difficult to assimilate the multiplicity of this strange land.

Reading her thoughts, Blake said, 'That's one place where East meets West—camels and Cadillacs.'

'It's incredible,' Lauren exclaimed wonderingly. 'Who lives there?'

'Foreign labourers mainly, and tribesmen.' Blake shrugged expressively. 'Great efforts have been made to rehabilitate the Bedouin, but they're nomadic by nature and as freedom is their most prized possession, it's something they won't give up lightly.' He continued reflectively. 'During my boyhood, I met an old Arab chieftain. I can see him now—picking up a handful of sand and letting it trickle through his fingers. *Each grain is a moment of happiness,* he told me. It was his way of expressing freedom.'

Lauren nodded perceptively. 'I can appreciate their sentiments, but it's difficult to believe how anyone can live under such conditions.'

'Everything has its opposite, Lauren,' Blake pointed out. 'Two sides of a coin. Good and evil. Life and death. Squalor and splendour.' His voice was charged with feeling. 'The East makes one more aware of these opposites—it shapes their philosophy.'

'That I can believe,' Lauren replied earnestly. She tilted her head and looked at him smilingly, her heart giving a little lift of joy. 'I'm glad you brought me this way,' she said, and thought again how wonderful it was to be spending the day with Blake Elliott.'

'Good,' Blake replied. His eyes passed over her like a slow caress, and a tingle of excitement shivered along her nerves.

As they drove along in companionable silence, Lauren

remembered fleetingly the proposed verbal battle. With a sense of relief, she realised that Blake had seemingly also forgotten, and she had no intention of reminding him of the challenge.

The track joined the main road and her interest quickened as the ruins of the ancient crenellated walls that had once fortified Quamat against marauding tribes appeared before them.

The road became congested with traffic. Trucks blustered their way alongside cars and the constant blaring of horns announced the presence of irate taxi-drivers. Donkeycarts got in the way of buses, and bicycles squeezed through whatever space they could find. The noise was deafening, and Lauren sighed with relief when Blake parked the car in the centre of Quamat.

'This is the Safat,' he explained, as he helped her out of the car. 'In bygone days it was the scene of public floggings, proclamations and the like. It's colourful at festival time.'

'I'm sure it is,' Lauren said, admiring the ancient square which for centuries had been the chief meeting place of the city. Caught up suddenly in the jostling crowd, she stumbled and, as Blake steadied her, he warned, 'Careful, girl. In this place, might has right.'

'So it would seem,' Lauren muttered, overwhelmed by the swarming crowd, then her natural good spirits came to the fore, and with twinkling eyes, she said to Blake, 'Well, come on, oh Mighty One, lead on. Where shall we start?'

Blake held her gaze, then grinned quizzically. 'Depends on your shopping list. Don't just say you want to look around. You could walk, become exhausted, then find we had to retrace our steps.'

'I want to see the bazaar,' Lauren said eagerly.

'Which one?' he asked dryly.

'All of them.' She looked up at him in amazement that he should find it necessary to ask. 'I want to see everything.'

Soon they were in the warren of narrow streets where

stalls were laden with merchandise. Elaborate leatherware vied with silks and brocades which were spread out like some fabulous rainbow. Expensive carpets were stacked in haphazard fashion. Tabriz, Kashan, Bokhara, Heraz, Khorassan—the names rolled off Blake's tongue like a poem.

As they wandered through the *suq*, the place was so full of impressions Lauren found it difficult to believe she was not turning the pages of a colourfully-illustrated book. Only the smells reminded her she was not. *They* were multifarious—leather and tobacco and rose-water intermingled with the odour of perspiring humanity. The atmosphere was one of noise and commotion.

At last Blake sent her an amused glance. 'A conducted tour is enough for one day, without Christmas shopping thrown in as a bonus. I don't know how you've persuaded me to do both.' He chuckled. 'Come on, my red-haired enchantress, let's head for Yussuf's. With a bit of luck, you can buy everything else there.'

Yussuf's store was a larger edition of Ghulam's shop at Maheil. The shelves were filled with an array of items that overwhelmed Lauren by their variety. She couldn't have had more choice in a London department store.

'This is terrific!' she exclaimed, staring in amazement at the modern-day Aladdin's cave.

'Do your shopping,' Blake suggested. 'I'll get some Pepsicola before we return to Akhmar. Sorry I can't invite you to lunch, but there's no Western restaurant as yet.'

'Okay,' Lauren chirped, and watched him stride towards the far end of the store before happily concentrating on choosing gifts for Christmas.

The sigh and sizzle of tyres moving on soft sand and the comfortable purring of the car engine induced a drowsiness in Lauren and soon her eyelids began to droop. When she opened them, the road seemed at a cross angle, and her head was resting comfortably on Blake's shoulder, his arm around her.

'Oh, I'm sorry. I didn't mean to go to sleep on you.'

'Physically, or otherwise?' His eyes were amused. 'Don't blush, it was my pleasure.' He sighed good-humouredly. 'We've certainly covered some ground today. Next time I take you to Quamat, we'll double the sightseeing and leave the shopping!'

Despite his good-natured threat, Lauren knew Blake had enjoyed the morning as much as she had done. In happiness, she wrinkled her nose.

On Christmas Eve, Lauren stood in front of the tree which she had helped Kath to decorate and her thoughts turned homewards. Christmas was a family time and she was missing her grandparents, the only family she had.

Kath had been dining with Ted and as she entered the lounge, she started waltzing around the room, arms outstretched, humming her favourite tune. Lauren knew her friend was in love with Ted, and was glad. Even in the little time Lauren had been in Akhmar, the plump, grey-eyed girl had found a special place in her heart, and she sincerely wished for Kath's happiness.

She smiled as Kath waltzed towards her.

'That man's fantastic, Lauren,' she rhapsodised, her voice slightly slurred. 'We've had a wonderful evening. Tomorrow we're spending Christmas at the hospital, but tonight has been ours.'

As if her legs could no longer support her, she flopped into her chair. 'Lauren,' she went on solemnly, 'I know you like Peter, and I know you like Blake—sometimes,' she nodded wisely. 'But remember, one is for kicks, the other is for keeps. Don't forget what your Auntie Kath has told you.' She tapped the side of her nose in such an absurd gesture that Lauren was unable to contain her laughter.

'Come on, my fine matchmaker,' Lauren told her. 'Bed! Otherwise you'll be too tired to enjoy tomorrow.'

Christmas Day dawned clear and bright. It seemed strange to think that, in Britain, pictures of snow and reindeer depicted the joyous season, yet here, in the land so far from her home, Lauren felt the ageless spirit of Christmas alight in her heart. She was filled with the joyousness of the bright day, and a curious contentment enveloped her.

As Kath emerged from the dining room, Lauren picked up the gold-link necklace she had purchased for Kath, and joyously the two girls exchanged gifts. Lauren was equally delighted with the musical powder bowl Kath had chosen for her.

Peter was spending a few day's local leave at Isfahan and had left a small package with instructions that Lauren was not to open it until Christmas morning. Now Lauren carefully opened the square box to reveal a beautiful gold fob-watch. 'Isn't this lovely, Kath?'

'It's super, Lauren.' Kath's grey eyes were solemn. 'That lad must like you a lot.'

'Yes, I rather think he does.' Lauren smiled and said candidly, 'But you know Peter! He's the sort of man one never takes seriously. You said so yourself.'

'People change,' Kath pointed out.

'They do indeed,' Lauren agreed, 'but Peter will always attract women.'

'Yes—and men like Peter are often the loneliest,' Kath remarked sagely. She admired the fob-watch again, then eyed Lauren speculatively. 'Don't you wish you could have gone with him?'

'Heavens, no,' Lauren said, much too quickly. 'I want to spend Christmas with Molly and the children.'

'Yes, of course you do, Lauren,' Kath replied softly, but even as she spoke, Lauren knew she was not deceived.

With a snap Lauren closed the box, feeling guilty because she really hadn't missed Peter very much at all.

She had fallen in love with Blake Elliott. In so doing, anyone else, even the handsome Peter Corbett, could claim nothing from her but friendship. She had nothing else to give. Her love was for Blake, and, ironically on this day of giving, it was the one gift she could not bestow.

A loud rap sounded on the outside door. Matthew, the Indian servant, went to answer it and suddenly the air became alive with excitement as his sing-song voice beckoned Kath to come quickly. Swiftly she walked to his aid. Lauren could hear murmured greetings in Arabic, then Kath invited the caller into the lounge.

The visitor was a tall dignified Arab clad in spotless white robes. He held himself with natural pride, but it was the gold medallion worn on a chain around his neck which gave him his authority. That medallion bore the insignia of the ruling family, and indicated that the man was a trusted servant.

'Miss Fletcher?' he enquired formally.

'Yes,' Lauren replied unwillingly, for the premonition that she had experienced at the cocktail party had now returned with compelling force. She watched in silence as the Arab bent low and touched his forehead in greeting.

'I am Khasim,' he told her. 'My master, the Sheikh Hassan, has entrusted me to deliver this gift,' he said proudly. He thrust his hand into the voluminous folds of his robe and withdrew an oblong case which he handed to Lauren with grave courtesy.

'Thank you,' said Lauren, taking the package from him, then feeling some further remark was called for, added with dignity, 'Please thank Sheikh Hassan for this honour he does me.'

'I will deliver your message most faithfully to my master,' he promised, and once more salaamed before leaving the bungalow. Bemused, the two girls stared at each other for confirmation that the scene they had witnessed had been no figment of their imagination.

Lauren gazed at the gift. Why had the Sheikh sent it to

her? Surely a smile at a cocktail party had little signifi-
cance. What could it mean? She had the sinking feeling
that it meant trouble. She saw her friend's astonished face
and, beckoning Kath to her side, she sat on the settee.

Her pulses raced as she undid the expensive wrapping to
disclose a green-velvet jewel case. Opening it reluctantly,
she gasped at the beauty of the emerald bracelet that lay
revealed in all its glittering splendour. Green flames leapt
from the square-cut stones and a blue glint flashing like
quicksilver emphasised the quality of the gems.

She stared at Kath in disbelief. 'Whatever shall I do with
it?'

'Put it on,' Kath said practically.

'That's an idea,' Lauren said more enthusiastically than
she felt, and carefully she placed the bracelet on her wrist.
It was beautiful and precious, yet its very presence reproached her.

'Gorgeous!' Kath rhapsodised.

'Kath,' Lauren said in awe, 'I'll have to work for a year
just to pay the insurance on something as valuable as this.'
She sighed. 'It's beautiful, but I can't keep it.' She bit her
lip. What should she do? She must see Blake. He would
advise her.

With that comforting thought, she took off the bracelet
and replaced it in the green velvet case.

When Lauren arrived at the Kennedy household, it was
evident that Santa Claus had been. Within minutes, the
twins were speaking to her twenty to the dozen, entreating
her to see *all* their presents. Molly introduced Timothy to
her.

Yes, he told her shyly, he enjoyed boarding school, but
he did miss his family.

Their conversation was cut short by the twins insisting
that she see their multitude of toys, but Molly chided them
with her forefinger.

'Now, now, children,' she told them, 'Auntie Lauren is going to be here all day, so don't tire her out in the first five minutes. Take a seat,' she insisted. 'Let me get you a sherry. Blake will be along later.'

'With Adele?' Lauren was unable to stop herself mentioning the nursing Sister, and she blushed furiously.

Molly looked puzzled. 'Adele's in Beirut.'

Lauren was about to ask her what Adele was doing in Beirut when Blake was in Akhmar. Surely they would want to be together—but really, it was no business of hers.

A door slammed, and the twins rushed to the door, shouting, 'Uncle Blake is here, Mummy. He's getting out of his car. We've told Daddy. He says he'll only be a minute. Do hurry up, Mummy, please!'

Blake's broad-shouldered frame seemed to fill the doorway. He placed a holdall at his side, then scooped up the twins, kissed Molly, called 'Happy Christmas, everyone,' and proceeded to shower them with gifts.

With her heart working overtime, Lauren undid the wrappings of her present. It was a superb model of an Arab sailing ship of striking appearance. Its graceful lines captured to the full the craftsman's art. Happiness pervaded her whole being, filling her with such joy, she could not have hidden her pleasure, even if she had wanted to. She bent her head quickly so Blake should not see her love for him written on her face. With care, she replaced the model in its box.

'Thank you, Blake. I'll treasure it always.'

With the word *treasure*, Lauren remembered Hassan's gift nestling in her handbag. She hadn't wanted to accept the bracelet, she told herself, yet common sense had made her realise it would be imprudent to return it to the Sheikh via his messenger. She shrugged nervously. She would ask Blake about it—later.

She looked up to make some casual remark, when she saw he was studying her thoughtfully.

'I'm glad you like it,' he said quietly. 'For the record, I also like you. Could the feeling be reciprocal?' The dark blue eyes searched her face.

Lauren's expression was calm, but her heart was banging against her ribs. 'Of course I like you,' she admitted, trying to keep the intensity out of her voice. It was such an ordinary phrase, yet it held all the passion that must remain unspoken. Her heart ached. She knew that sooner or later she was going to be hurt. She met Blake's gaze unwaveringly. Let the hurt come later. Today was today, and Christmas Day at that.

'Merry Christmas, Blake,' she said, and handed him the gift she had chosen, a copy of A. E. Housman's *A Shropshire Lad*.

As their fingers touched, Lauren felt every nerve she possessed become alive. She knew her body housed a network of electric wires that were gradually building up a tremendous overload that would explode outwards.

Suddenly Blake spoke, and his voice was curiously impressive. 'The Arabs pat hands to seal a contract, but I prefer this way,' and stooping forward, he kissed her lightly on the lips. 'Thanks—for so many things, Lauren.'

'And you too, Blake,' she whispered, aware that her personal power generator was getting overloaded by the minute.

The cook surpassed himself with the Christmas lunch— turkey and all the trimmings, plum pudding alight with brandied flames, mince pies, crackers and paper hats. The children gave the day a special pleasure. Lauren smiled at Molly and Alan, secure in their family joy, and knew it to be a day well blessed.

All too soon it was time to say goodnight. Blake offered to drive Lauren home and, after thanking their hosts, they stepped on to the verandah and walked towards the car parked in the driveway. A cool breeze rippled through the leaves of the oleanders making a sound like the sea washing the shore. Lauren was sorry the day had to end.

With that uncanny knack he had of reading her thoughts, Blake murmured, 'Pity to end the evening. What about a drive?'

'Mmm! That would be lovely,' she agreed. 'Where did you have in mind?'

'There's a nice stretch of beach at Maheil.'

'Sounds ideal.'

'Okay.' Blake laid a hand on her arm and smiled an invitation. 'Let's go!'

They drove over the old desert road, past *serifa* settlements made ghostly and mysterious by the flickering kerosene lanterns that hung in shadowed doorways. About ten minutes later they reached the outskirts of Maheil. With a contented sigh, Blake pulled the car into a half-circle, and parked overlooking the water.

Leaving the car, they started walking along the deserted beach. The ancient waters of the Gulf lapped quietly on the shore, reminding Lauren of the swishing of a silken gown. The moon, bright and clear, bathed everything in unreality. There was a softness about the light, more noticeable after the harsh quality of the sharp sunlight of the day.

At last they stopped, and with one arm around Lauren's shoulder, Blake pointed to the heavens. 'Look up there,' he said, and at his bidding, Lauren gazed into the star-studded sky.

'Yes?' she said tremulously.

'Just over there, beneath that constellation, lies Bethlehem,' he told her.

'Bethlehem,' Lauren repeated. The night seemed full of mystery, of strange, inexplicable designs, incomprehensible to man, making Lauren feel she was but a mere speck in the universe.

Over there lay Bethlehem. It was a soul-lifting experience for Lauren. She knew with a knowledge that came from some unseen source that this was all part of her life. Somehow she was a stranger at the gate, and the gate had opened and let her in.

'Are you all right?' Blake asked, strangely quiet as if he sensed that she was deeply moved by this night full of symbolism.

'I'm fine,' she said, and lifted her hands in a simple gesture. 'I've been trying to come to terms with all this—Man and the universe, so to speak. It makes me realise how insignificant I am.'

'You're not insignificant to me.' Blake bent his head low and she felt the lingering pressure of warm firm lips. At his gentle caress, she felt herself sinking and strove to find some rescue spar before she was drowned in desire for this man.

Adele! How can he kiss me like this when he's going to marry Adele? Abruptly, Lauren turned her face away.

Blake caught her by the shoulders, his fingers biting into her skin. 'What the hell are you playing at, Lauren?' he asked aggressively. 'I gained the impression you were enjoying that kiss—so what gives?'

'A kiss is a kiss,' Lauren answered flippantly, hating every word she uttered. With a tremendous effort of will, she looked him full in the face. 'No one gets serious out here,' she said coquettishly. 'Not even you. You're going to marry Adele—yet you flirt with me!'

'So you think that, do you, Lauren?' She flinched at the expression in his eyes. 'You certainly haven't a high opinion of me, that's for sure. So I'm going to marry Adele?' His eyes narrowed. 'I find that interesting.'

'That's what I heard,' Lauren retorted, her nails dug into the palms of her hands, and she wished she was anywhere but on the beach at Maheil.

'And you're so trusting, you believe everything you hear,' Blake went on relentlessly. 'Thanks for your vote of confidence. I thought better of you, Lauren, but I should have known you were too good to be true.'

Lauren clenched her fists. 'I don't think you need preach about anyone!'

'I'll preach about anyone I damn well like,' he retorted.

'When I think of you, all pride and purity, I could spit. You don't know what it is to trust people,' he taunted her. 'You've been let down once, so, as far as you're concerned, all men are tarred with the same brush.' He drew in a sharp breath. 'Well, go ahead and have a ball. There's any number of men who'll only be too glad to partner you, and to hell with the consequences. In a community where men outnumber women twenty to one, you get that sort of attitude. Don't worry, I won't kiss you again. I value my self-respect too much.' He gave a short, mirthless laugh. 'Come on, the party's over. Let's get back to the car.'

Numbed by the reaction of his words, Lauren stumbled blindly towards the car. Pride would have made her walk, but sanity prevailed. She would soon get lost in the alien world the desert became at night. She got into the car, managing to control the sob that threatened to wreck her self-control. If Blake had wanted to hurt her, he had succeeded. Silently she slid into her seat, then, unable to keep quiet, she flared, 'You can talk, but you're like all the others —even sheikhs!'

'What the hell have sheikhs got to do with it?' Blake demanded angrily, and she felt the hard grip of his hand on her arm.

'Oh, didn't I tell you,' Lauren said flippantly, 'Hassan sent me this by special messenger this morning.' Defiantly, she plucked the jewel-case from her handbag and opened it to show him the glittering emeralds.

'You accepted this from Hassan?' Blake's voice was an accusation. 'Don't you know what you've done? You little fool! You damned little fool!'

'I didn't ask for the bracelet,' Lauren stormed, turning to face him. 'Anyway, I intended returning it to Hassan, but I didn't think it the height of tact to return it via his servant.'

'Quite right,' Blake rasped, turning the key in the ignition.

'How nice to be right,' Lauren retorted bitterly. 'Am I supposed to thank you for that crumb of comfort?'

Ignoring her sarcasm, Blake continued, his voice silky and dangerously quiet. 'Don't you know that to return a gift to an Arab is tantamount to an insult?' He paused to let his words sink in. 'Oil companies don't take kindly to their Arab friends being insulted—so you won't exactly be in their good books.'

'Thanks for the compliment,' Lauren snapped, and wished she didn't feel so physically sick. With a superhuman effort, she lit a cigarette and gazed unseeingly out of the windscreen.

He scowled. 'Damn Hassan! I should have known he'd do something like this.' His lips tightened and his voice was charged with feeling as he added, 'I'm seeing him tomorrow, so leave it with me.'

'What are you going to tell him?' Lauren swung round to face him, her green eyes glittering with suppressed emotion. Things seemed to be getting out of hand. She had not intended to sail in waters as deep as this.

'What I tell Hassan is my concern,' Blake snapped. 'You want the gift returning. Right?'

'Right, first time,' Lauren snapped back, angry with herself for turning the evening into a nightmare. It had been such a lovely day. Why hadn't they said goodnight at the Kennedys'? And why had she been able to kiss Blake with gay abandon without having the thought of Adele on her conscience?

Blake lit a cigarette and the lighter flared, briefly illuminating the angry, chiselled profile. Abruptly he turned to her and said, 'Well, it's been a memorable Christmas Day, I'll grant you that, Lauren.' He heaved an exaggerated sigh. 'Glory me! Now I know why that old toolpusher from Texas advised me never to tangle with females. Life sure gets complicated when they're around.' He gave her a look of scorn. 'Especially you. In comparison, oil rigs are angels.'

Lauren was too exhausted for further emotional sparring, so wisely she stayed silent.

Blake glanced at the luminous dial of his watch. 'How appropriate,' he murmured sarcastically. 'It's Boxing Day!'

Nothing Lauren could say could cap a remark like that, so she sighed unhappily, and reflected that it had not been such a merry Christmas after all.

CHAPTER EIGHT

HOLIDAYS over, Lauren returned to work. Three days elapsed and she had not seen or heard from Blake. However hard she tried to concentrate on the job in hand, her thoughts were like shadows that chased each other endlessly down an ever-familiar corridor. What had Blake said to Hassan? How had Hassan reacted? Until she could see Blake and hear his solution, she had no way of knowing, and the agony of waiting made every task she had to perform an irritation.

As luck would have it, she was out of the office when Blake did appear and she returned to find him standing by her desk. He was whistling a popular tune and looked carefree and relaxed.

'Good morning, Blake,' she said eagerly. 'Did you enjoy the hunting trip?'

'Yes, thanks, very much.'

'Well, what happened?'

'About what?' he countered.

'Oh, Blake,' she pleaded, trying not to appear too exasperated. 'You know I'm waiting to hear what happened when you returned the bracelet to Hassan, yet here we are talking about trivialities!'

'Flattering to know you consider working for me a triviality.' He shrugged deprecatingly. 'It's something you're going to have to put up with for a little longer, I'm afraid. Mr Stewart isn't returning until February.' His face gave nothing away, but his voice reproached her. 'As to the bracelet, Hassan has it.'

'Oh! I'm so glad,' Lauren's relief was considerable. 'What did he say?'

'He accepted my explanation.'

'And that was?'

'That I disapproved.'

'But you must have said something else,' Lauren retorted impatiently. Exasperation made her want to take him by the shoulders and shake the information out of him, but she was incapable of such a physical feat. Instead she said heatedly, 'I can't see Hassan taking kindly to your disapproval. After all, the whole object of the exercise was to lessen his displeasure.'

Her words electrified Blake into action. He squared his shoulders and, when he spoke, it was very tersely. 'The whole idea of returning the jewellery was to get you out of a situation which could have led to serious consequences.'

'What do you mean by that?' Lauren flashed.

'I should have thought it obvious even to a person with your naivety,' he snapped. 'It's about time you grew up, Lauren.' The expression on his face made her want to hit him.

'Mr Elliott,' she said, with as much dignity as she could muster, 'I'm not a child straight out of the nursery and I dislike intensely the implication of your remarks. I do, however, find it difficult to believe that Hassan would accept the return of the bracelet without some justifiable explanation.'

'He had the best reason in the world,' Blake replied poker-faced, 'I told him I intend to marry you.'

'Marry me?' Lauren exploded. 'You must be joking!'

At Blake's solemn gaze, she was shocked into silence. The clash of conflict once again made her heart pound unbearably. By the very nature of his remark, he was making a mockery of her dreams, and she hated him for it.

'Whatever you told Hassan, Mr Elliott,' she said stiffly, 'I still have to thank you for your efforts on my behalf. It would have been most awkward for me to return the gift.' Indignation rose afresh in her. 'However, I consider your last remark in extremely bad taste.'

Blake looked at her impassively.

She stood there, wishing she could correctly interpret the expression in his eyes. She bristled and bent her head so he would not see her trembling, busying herself with checking appointments. She hoped he would take the hint and go away. Instead the action evidently provoked him, and he leaned forward and said sarcastically, 'Don't let the matter of our future marriage stop you working. Such zeal is commendable.' He placed a firm hand over hers. 'As a matter of fact, the hunting trip has blown away the cobwebs, so I'm ready to tackle the paperwork.' His grip tightened. 'Let's start,' he said, and when Lauren looked up at him, she felt defeated.

'Certainly, Mr Elliott,' she replied coolly and, moving her hand, she picked up her notebook and went ahead of him into the inner sanctum.

Later she saw the director's cablegram referring to his delayed return. It would be pleasant to see Mr Stewart again. Yet once he returned, the less she would see of Blake. But wasn't that what she wanted? Why, then, did the future seem bleak? Impatient with herself, puzzled by Blake's reaction, she found solace in concentrating on her notes.

Blake returned to sign papers late the following afternoon. As he put his signature to the last document, he said abruptly, 'I suppose you're going to celebrate New Year's Eve at the dance tonight?'

'Yes,' Lauren admitted defensively.

'With the admirable Mr Corbett?'

'That's right, Mr Elliott.'

Blake stroked his chin thoughtfully, then said as if he had some doubts on the matter, 'I'm sure you'll have a most enjoyable evening.'

Lauren simmered. He was making it sound as if she were embarking on some hazardous expedition, instead of attending a festive occasion with a handsome young man.

'It's my intention to have an enjoyable evening.' She knew she sounded aggressive, and resented the fact that

Blake made her react in such a fashion. Talk about biological chicanery!

'You know what they say about intentions,' Blake replied, a half-smile playing at the corner of his lips. Lauren had the absurd desire to tease him and say, 'No, I don't—please tell me.' Instead, she stifled the impulse and murmured, 'Goodnight, Mr Elliott.'

With the signed papers in her hand, she moved towards the door.

'Goodnight, Miss Fletcher,' Blake replied formally, then, picking up his cigarettes from the desk, placed them in his shirt pocket and made ready to leave. Before Lauren understood what was happening, he was at the door ahead of her and, looking down at her with tolerant amusement, he tilted her chin and kissed her lightly on the lips. 'That's to wish you a Happy New Year. I'm dining with the general manager, so I won't be at the dance tonight.' He grinned, 'Enjoy yourself, and don't forget to make a resolution to count to ten before you blow your top! Goodnight, Lauren.'

Stupefied, Lauren stared at his retreating figure, forgetful of all else except the whispered kiss on her lips, the merriment dancing in his blue eyes, and the surge of disappointment that flooded through her as she realised he would not be at the dance to welcome in the New Year.

In the end, the dance proved to be a somewhat slow affair, despite Peter's entertaining account of his holiday in Isfahan.

Caught up in the crowd of people singing Auld Lang Syne, Lauren remembered, with a yearning intensity, Blake's light kiss, and found it hurt unbearably to think of the future, deprived of his love.

Winter came upon the oil town overnight, shattering Lauren with its severity. If anyone had told her in the warmth of October that soon she would be shivering with cold, she would not have believed them, yet here she was now wearing thick sweaters and skirts, and huddling inside her anorak. The Arab women wore heavy clothing under their *abayahs*, while the children put on sweaters over their *dishdasha* and wrapped their heads in woollen scarves. Mohammed, the driver, wore a checked sports jacket over his robes—another example of East meeting West, Lauren thought wryly.

She was aware that, for Blake, the weather only produced more problems at the rigs, as severe weather conditions caused stoppages and equipment failure, which were due to the two extremes of temperature—a touch of frost during the night and early morning, then climbing to the mid-nineties in the middle of the day. He was beginning to look extremely fatigued. The usually bronzed skin seemed to have turned white, as if drawn too tightly over the cheekbones, giving his eyes a strained appearance. He was doing two jobs at once and, between them, the long hours were beginning to stretch nerve and sinew. Lauren wanted to tell him a full night's sleep would do him the world of good, but she knew such a remark would be met with a satirical reply.

It was one such morning she handed him his usual cup of coffee. He emptied it in one gulp and asked for a second cup. As she returned with a refill. Lauren's fingers tightened around the cup as she saw Blake holding the receiver of the red telephone.

'Hell!' he said, slamming down the receiver. 'Drink the coffee yourself. I'm off to Rig Five.'

'That Rig Five,' Lauren thought worriedly, 'doesn't give a body any rest.' As she drank the coffee, she wondered uneasily what the problem was this time. Hours passed, and at four o'clock she decided there was nothing she could do so she headed for home.

As soon as Lauren walked into the lounge, her anxiety about Rig Five was pushed aside. There was that curious stillness about the room that one senses when all is not well. The tea-trolley, laid for tea, she noticed, was untouched.

She stood still, listening, and from the direction of Kath's room she could hear the sound of muffled sobs. Moving quickly, she tapped lightly on Kath's door.

'Kath,' she called. 'Are you all right?'

'Fine,' came the muffled reply.

'You don't sound it.' Without further ado, Lauren entered the bedroom to find her friend sitting huddled in a chair. Kath's face was blotchy, her eyes red-rimmed from weeping.

Concerned, Lauren placed her arm around Kath's shoulders. 'Kath,' she asked anxiously, 'whatever is the matter?'

Kath sniffed and muttered an inaudible reply that Lauren interpreted as '*Men!*'

'But what's wrong?' Lauren probed. She waited for Kath to tell her, but instead she began to cry again. 'Come on, poppet, mop up,' she urged. 'Things can't be that bad.'

Gradually Kath's sobbing subsided and she took a handkerchief from her pocket. 'Sorry, Lauren. Not like me to get so emotional.' Her grey eyes were solemn. 'I guess I've never been in love before.'

'Ted ... Is he all right?'

'Yes. That is, he's not sick or anything, but we've had an awful row.' She was ready to cry again, but controlled the outburst. 'About a month ago I saw him talking to Adele in the main corridor of the hospital. Since then I'm always bumping into them. Today, I interrupted what was obviously a personal conversation.' Kath clasped Lauren's hand. 'Oh, Lauren,' she wailed, 'I know I shouldn't have asked him, but I couldn't help myself.'

'What did you ask him?' Lauren said patiently.

'If Adele means anything to him.'

'And what did Ted say?' Lauren prompted.

Kath bent her head, her hand tightening on Lauren's arm. 'He wouldn't answer, but remarked that people have to live their own lives. That made me feel guilty about probing into his personal affairs, so I told him I heartily endorse such beliefs.' She laughed, but it was a hollow laughter. 'I also told him that most people I knew were reluctant to give up their independence, and didn't he know I lead the parade in that respect.' Her mouth quivered. 'It's that wretched Adele. She can't leave any man alone. She's got to ensnare every man she meets, and when she's captured their affections, she doesn't give a fig.'

'I'm sure it's not as bad as you make out, Kath,' Lauren consoled her friend. 'All couples have rows. My guess is Ted's feeling just as upset as you, and just as unhappy. Things will be all right, I'm sure.'

'Thanks, Lauren,' said Kath, but she didn't sound hopeful. She stared into the dressing-table mirror. 'Gosh, I look an awful sight! I'll bathe my face, then I'll join you for tea.'

'Okay,' Lauren smiled. 'Don't be long. I'll ask Matthew to brew a fresh pot.'

She sighed. With women like Adele, paradise would never be regained. Down the centuries, beautiful and wicked women had captured men's affections. Why should it be so? She shrugged impatiently. Men were fools when it came to love. With that thought, she closed her eyes and pictured the raven-haired Adele—and the mental image was not reassuring. She hoped Ted wasn't seriously interested in the nursing Sister. The idea perturbed her, not because she cared about Adele, or even Ted, but Kath was the sort of person who didn't fall in love easily. If she didn't marry Ted, then she would never marry anyone—she would become the favourite aunt and care for her sisters' children, instead of her own. With that sober judgement, Lauren drank her tea, and wondered what the morning would bring.

Next day the office seemed strangely quiet. Joseph was off sick and by ten o'clock Blake had not appeared. Alert to every movement, Lauren's attention was caught by an unfamiliar noise in the inner office. The door opened and there stood the general manager.

'Mr Elliott?' he enquired.

'He hasn't come in yet, sir. Yesterday, Mr Elliott received an emergency call. He was going to Rig Five, but so far no message has come through.'

'That's interesting,' commented the general manager. He smiled at Lauren. 'This is something you'll have to get used to with Mr Elliott—drilling, and all its many facets, are life's blood to him, after all.' Shrewdly he looked at the slender girl, and noticed her anxiety. 'It may not be serious,' he said kindly. 'I'll find out what's going on and let you know.'

Lauren thanked him, and found comfort in thinking that Adele wasn't going to find it all that easy to persuade Blake to take up the appointment in London.

Eventually the general manager returned. 'You've had a long day, Miss Fletcher, but now you can relax. Mr Elliott will be at the rig for at least three days, snatching sleep when he can, so don't disturb him for anything. If there are problems, come to me.'

'Yes, sir. Thank you.' Hesitantly, she enquired, 'What's the trouble?'

'Loss of circulation. It's serious, but it's also a challenge.' Lauren could have sworn his eyes twinkled. 'Between you and me, Mr Elliott will enjoy every minute of it, then come back tired but triumphant, drink too much, sleep for forty-eight hours, and come bounding back as though nothing had happened.' He smiled. 'That will be the time to ask him all about it.'

At his words, Lauren remembered he had been an oil man all his life. Looking at him, feeling his concern and understanding of the situation, she knew why he was a great man in the world of great men.

He smiled again. 'For the moment, my dear, my advice to you is relax. When Mr Elliott returns, there'll be so much work for you to do, you'll need a pressure relief valve fitted to your typewriter! Goodnight.'

'Goodnight, sir, and thank you.'

The next three days seemed like an intermittent dream and one day swirled into the greyness of the other. Then, on the morning of the fourth day, Lauren looked up suddenly to find Blake standing in the doorway. She stood up quickly.

'I know,' she quavered. 'Coffee.'

'Gallons.'

'Right away!'

After Blake had emptied his cup for the third time, Lauren said thankfully, 'I'm glad you're back. The general manager told me the problem was loss of circulation. How does that happen?'

'Take a seat, and I'll explain.'

Lauren sat facing him, and inwardly insisted that her heart behave and not be diverted by the awareness of the man sitting opposite her.

Blake lit a cigarette and then proceeded to explain. 'During drilling operations,' he told her, 'we use what's known in the trade as "mud" mixed to a density which is always greater than the known well pressure. Problems occur when a hole, or fracture, in the formation is encountered, and instead of the mud circulating and returning to the surface for re-treatment, it disappears. It's costly, and we can't afford to push tons of this mud into the depths of the earth, so the fracture has to be sealed off.' He shrugged. 'This can be done in numerous ways—no need to go into that aspect this morning. The biggest danger, however, is that when there's not a column of mud in the well to hold back the pressure, a sudden kick from the well could certainly cause a blow-out, carrying with it the danger of fire.'

Lauren said shyly, 'Thanks for explaining. It makes typing technical reports that much easier to understand,' she told him.

Blake eyed her thoughtfully. 'You like your work, don't you? Oh, not just the secretarial side, but the oil industry itself?'

'It's fabulous,' said Lauren, then added with a hint of

cheekiness, 'I've heard it said if you stay long enough, you get oil in your veins.'

Blake said dryly, 'I would rather say that the blood in your veins is changed to oil.'

'I can believe that. The oil industry is a world on its own. Once you get caught up in it, it swamps you like some great industrial tide.' Lauren grinned. 'Pay's good, too!'

'We're paid for what we're worth.' Blake sounded suddenly exhausted as if reaction was setting in after the efforts of the last few days.

On impulse, Lauren said, 'Why don't you head for home and catch up on your sleep?'

'That's a good idea—only one thing wrong with it.'

'What's that?' Lauren asked innocently.

'No delectable female to hold my hand. Pity!'

Lauren was rendered speechless. She watched him rise wearily from his chair, pick up his cigarettes, and heard him say, 'Tell the general manager I'm sleeping myself back to sanity. He'll understand.'

Lauren nodded. 'I'll do that.'

'Good.' He stood for a moment as if intending to add to his comment, but, deciding otherwise, he gave a tired smile and left the office.

Lauren listened to his footsteps echoing down the corridor, and returned to her desk with a lightness of heart she had not thought possible since the incident of the bracelet. As for Blake's comment to Hassan that he intended to marry her, she had reached the conclusion that Blake had made the remark on the spur of the moment, knowing Hassan would accept such an explanation.

If only Blake had really meant it—Lauren sighed and made her way home, cheered by the knowledge that she and Blake were no longer at loggerheads.

Kath had also recovered her cheerful spirits. She and Ted were again seeing each other. The gloom that had followed her flood of tears had been dispelled, and Lauren's fears that Adele might complicate what seemed to be a promising relationship, happily appeared groundless. Kath had also mentioned that she and Ted had had a long talk. She didn't enlarge on their conversation, and Lauren didn't probe. The important thing was to see Kath happy.

That evening the two girls decided to do something about their costumes for the fancy dress ball, which was to be held at the Dolphin Club on St Valentine's Day.

They finished sewing their costumes only the day before the ball, and the day of the ball found them in a whirl of excitement as they dressed for the masquerade.

Kath was ready and went to show Lauren the maroon gown which she had chosen to wear in her masquerade of Elizabeth Barrett Browning.

'Well, how do I look?' Kath asked shyly.

'You look lovely, Kath,' Lauren told her. 'If your name-sake looked as beautiful as you do tonight, no wonder Robert Browning proposed!'

Kath glowed. 'This gown you designed for me does do wonders for my figure, doesn't it?'

'Yes,' Lauren assured her, 'and as Ted is going as Robert Browning, let's hope history repeats itself.'

'I hope so,' Kath whispered, and her face was radiant at the thought.

Lauren gave herself a critical look in the mirror. Her costume was a gown of green velvet. It contrived to give the impression of having seen better days, yet nevertheless it was attractive and accentuated the slimness of her figure and was a perfect foil for her hair and skin. With a shawl around her shoulders, a large hat crowned with flowers perched on her head, a flower-seller's basket clutched in her hand, Lauren reflected that Eliza Doolittle was ready for the ball.

'Let's hope you meet Professor Higgins,' Kath giggled. 'You look enchanting, but you'll have to mind your language.'

'Too bloody right!' Lauren grinned. 'That there Peter is going as Sir Lancelot.'

The two girls were still laughing when Peter and Ted Massey arrived. The visual approval of their escorts was all they needed, and it was a happy foursome that made its way to the Dolphin Club.

The ballroom was decorated with paper-chains, balloons and Victorian silhouettes which some artistic soul had stuck all over the place. In the centre of the ceiling, a huge multi-coloured globe revolved and the jewelled lights, flickering in the darkness, accompanied by a haunting melody, gave an air of romance to the occasion and made friends, dressed in their unfamiliar costume, appear strange and exciting.

Peter had reserved a table at the edge of the dance floor. He had just ordered drinks and was talking to Kath and Ted when he stopped suddenly, whistled softly and waved. Following his gaze, Lauren saw Adele.

The nursing Sister was dressed as Cleopatra, and looked breathtakingly beautiful in a gown of gold. Her hair had been elaborately coiffured, her make-up impeccable, and the result was simply spectacular. Yet for all her beauty, Lauren sensed something secretive about her, some feline characteristic that could prove dangerous.

Acknowledging Peter's wave, she moved towards him. 'Hello, darling,' she greeted him—her husky voice making the endearment vital and personal.

Peter stood up and gave a mock bow. 'You look marvellous, Adele,' he enthused, admiring her without restraint.

Adele acknowledged his praise with an arrogant shrug. 'You look rather good yourself, Peter darling,' she cooed, then she glanced at Lauren. 'And what have we here—a waif from the streets of London?' She laughed, amused at her own description.

'Me a waif—and you a queen. Completely different in so many ways.' Lauren made the words expressly ambiguous.

Adele frowned and turned her attention to Kath and Ted. 'Ah, the poet lovers, I see. How droll!'

At Adele's remarks, Kath coloured fiercely, but before she could speak, Lauren interposed, 'I'd say Robert Browning found greater happiness than Mark Antony—wouldn't you, Adele?'

Adele's lips tightened into a thin, unattractive line, but she didn't deign to answer.

Unrelenting, Lauren continued her attack, saying with pretended innocence, 'I must say, Adele, your costume certainly steals the limelight.'

Adele preened. 'I'm rather pleased with it myself.' She shrugged contemptuously. 'Of course, the limelight isn't the right setting for everyone.'

'I agree,' Lauren demurred, then followed up her attack. 'The trouble is, of course, the limelight also shows up the flaws.'

Adele drew herself up to her full height and retorted arrogantly, 'Don't worry for yourself, dear—limelight isn't exactly your scene.' She smiled scornfully. 'Excuse me, Blake will be waiting,' and nodding to the rest of the party, she walked away with an abruptness that was almost rude.

Peter stared after her in perplexity. 'What was all that about? Do tell me if there's something I should know.'

Lauren said softly, 'It was nothing, Peter. A feminine whim, if you like.' Her voice trailed as she watched Adele approach Blake, who appeared to be searching for her.

To Lauren's eyes, Blake was the most distinguished man in the room. He was wearing what appeared to be the dress uniform of a British regiment, and the scarlet-and-gold apparel only served to accentuate his dark, attractive looks. Yet the bright jacket, the military precision of the black trousers, conveyed a subtle hint that while he was joining in the merriment of the occasion, he was not a man to make a fool of himself by dressing up in some ridiculous garb.

As Lauren watched him gaze at Adele with obvious admiration, the sight of him filled her with a terrible hunger that she had never before experienced. It was a hunger for some abstract fulfilment that she could not put into words. All that she had ever wanted out of life, believed in, dreamed about, was wrapped up in that ball of hunger that was now becoming a tight knot of despair as her wayward thoughts returned to reality.

She continued watching Blake, and willed that he look at her. To her amazement, he stared across the room as if he had listened in to her thoughts. Slowly, he walked towards her, Adele unwillingly following in his wake.

Amusement danced in the dark blue eyes as he appraised Lauren's waif-like appearance. 'Miss Doolittle, I presume? May I say how charming you look?'

'So quaint, don't you think, Blake,' Adele said with silky gentleness. 'The perfect flower-girl.'

'Good evening, Major Elliott,' Lauren said impishly. 'May I say what a handsome military man you make?'

Blake eyed her suspiciously, then recognising the impishness in her manner, joined in her laughter.

Adele interrupted. 'Have you met Dr Edward Massey, Blake?'

Blake smiled. 'Briefly.' The two men shook hands. 'I think we have a mutual friend, Dr Massey. John Frost?'

'Dr Frost, you mean?'

'That's the chap. I met him at El Rubai.'

'He's my cousin,' said Ted, and Lauren sensed a tension flicker in the air, but had no time to dwell on it, for Adele entered the conversation.

'Frost is a common name,' she said, and linked her arm through Blake's as if to detract his attention from the group.

'In the oil world, one's always meeting mutual friends,' Peter remarked, and Blake surprisingly nodded assent.

'Quite so,' Ted replied, and gazed at Adele. Lauren hoped he wouldn't be hypnotised by the modern-day Cleopatra. Adele Harding was a creature men would find hard to resist. 'But not Ted,' she willed, and was glad to hear Blake say,

'How lovely you look, Kath. Positively radiant,' Kath's glow of happiness at Blake's compliment was evident. 'Happy party you have here,' Blake went on, and looked as if he hoped he would be invited to join the group.

'It certainly is a happy party,' Peter echoed Blake's words. For once, there seemed to be no coolness between him and Blake.

Ted invited Blake and Adele to join the party. Blake seemed pleased at the invitation, but Adele said petulantly, 'One drink, perhaps,' and when a waiter brought a fresh supply of drinks, she picked up a glass and drawled, 'Champagne! My, you are celebrating.'

'Yes,' Lauren said cryptically. 'We're drinking to Women's Lib.'

Adele was not amused and drummed her deep-red lacquered fingernails in a rapid staccato on the table top.

Kath said softly, 'Hush, Lauren. Drink your champagne.'

'I have a better idea,' said Blake, taking Lauren's glass and placing it on the table. 'They're playing my favourite waltz. Let's dance.'

'I'd love to,' Lauren said breathlessly, and as Blake gripped her arm to guide her to the dance floor, she saw that Adele's amber eyes glinted with malice. Apprehension flicked the nape of her neck like a cold wind and she knew that Adele would not hesitate to cause mischief if she were given an opportunity.

Vaguely, she heard Peter ask Adele to dance, but as Blake put his arms around her, she became caught up in the magic of the waltz and all else was forgotten.

As if dancing in a dream, she relaxed and let herself float on the sea of sound, not wanting anything to disturb the pure happiness she felt at that moment. With almost a physical start, she became aware of Blake saying softly, 'You're as beautiful as your flowers, Eliza.'

Lauren smiled up into his face, and, liking what she saw there, she gave way to the impulse to tease him. 'Thank you, Major Elliott, but they will surely wilt unless they're cared for.'

'I'm sure that can be arranged,' Blake whispered, and Lauren swallowed quickly to disperse the emotional pull of her thoughts.

'In what way?' she asked breathlessly.

He grinned easily. 'The swimming pool is still full—water there be, if water is needed. In with the lot—including Eliza Doolittle.'

'Oh, Major Elliott, sir,' Lauren stammered, 'you wouldn't take advantage of a poor girl?'

He gripped her tightly around the waist. 'If she's beautiful, I wouldn't hesitate,' and Lauren didn't know whether to believe him or not. He added softly, 'And more especially if she happens to be a red-headed minx.'

Lauren took a deep breath. 'In that case, Major,' she whispered seductively, 'I'm glad I fit such a description.' She could feel his grip tighten, his breathing alter perceptibly, and encouraged by the champagne she had sipped, retorted, 'And I must say, I think you look more handsome as a military man than as a roughneck.'

Blue eyes met green and exchanged merriment—and something else. An elusive will-o'-the-wisp quality darted back and forth between them. They stopped their laughter and stared at each other as if seeing one another for the very first time.

I'll remember this moment for ever, Lauren told herself. She wanted to shut everything out of her mind but the sound of music weaving in and out, filling her with exultation; enjoying the exquisite agony of being held close by the man she loved. Yet she knew she must break the spell. She must withstand the emotion caused by the music, her imagination and the nearness of Blake, or she would betray herself—and that would never do. Blake was not for her, and she would do well to remember it.

'You're trembling,' he said, and she studied his face with a quick ache in her throat.

'It's only the excitement of the evening,' she lied. 'It's my first fancy dress ball.'

'Then we must see it's not your last.' Blake's voice, which had fascinated her from the first, now sent a shiver along her nerve-ends, and she had to steady the impulse to respond wholeheartedly to his masculinity. She stiffened slightly and said with determined coolness,

'Did you know that Lauren means laurel leaf?'

'Gift to the victor, perhaps?'

'Victory is not always sweet, my friend,' she answered, and felt a fever begin within her.

At the unexpectedness of her reply, Blake looked puzzled. The increased pressure of his fingers in the small of her back made her feel breathless. With a smothered feeling in her throat, she waited for him to speak. Instead his dark eyes searched her own as if to find some answer there.

With defiance, she returned his gaze, and she knew he thought she played some game with him. There was a curious look on Blake's face which she could not identify. She had an intense yearning to stop dancing, to stretch out her hand, touch his face and tell him whatever had happened was a long time ago, that such painful memories were best forgotten. As the dark eyes held hers, a quiver of vulnerability shot through her and she again felt physical desire stir, and leap in response to Blake's undeniable magnetism. The music stopped, and she shrugged away the feeling and told herself that she had tasted too much wine.

When they returned to the table, Kath gave Blake a wide, friendly smile. 'Why don't you join us, Blake?'

'That's very kind of you,' he started to say, and Lauren sensed he was intent on refusing when Adele returned with Peter. Her face was upturned in laughter, her expression bright with conquest.

Molly and Alan joined the party, more champagne was ordered and, as Lauren picked up the glass of golden liquid placed before her, she shot a sideways glance at Blake. How remote he seemed! Had she imagined that strange quality of mutual magnetism as they had waltzed together?

As if sensing her gaze, Blake gave her a searching look, then he sipped his champagne and, after placing the empty glass on the table, asked Adele to dance.

Lauren bent her head, hoping no one would notice how

perilously close to tears she was. Her head ached. The babble of voices had exploded into an amplified echo of noise.

'Lauren, didn't you hear what I said?' Peter's voice was petulant.

'Sorry, Peter,' she said with a trace of apology. 'Tell me again.'

'I asked if you'd noticed that chunky opal on Adele's right hand. The rumour is circulating that she's become engaged.' He flashed a meaningful glance towards the dance floor. 'No need to wonder who the lucky man is!'

'You know what people say about rumours,' Lauren answered, and her voice sounded strange and low. The 'lucky man' would be Blake. It was no more than she had expected—yet reality, when it struck, was painful.

She felt herself caught up in a vortex of confused emotions and, struggling to gain her composure, she realised she had no alternative but to accept the situation.

In'shallah, the Arabs said. Everything was the will of Allah, but how strong-minded you had to be in order to believe in such a philosophy, especially when the pearly light of a magnificent opal stayed in one's inner vision, weakening one's resolve.

Blake and Adele were undeniably the most attractive couple in the room. As they circled the dance floor, a shattering sadness arose in Lauren's throat, spread in waves across her face, touched her eyes with unshed tears, and she knew herself to be a woman without belief, and realised, once more, that the sweet joys of loving were not for her.

CHAPTER NINE

AFTER that declaration from Peter that he believed Adele and Blake to be secretly engaged, Lauren relentlessly drove thoughts of what might have been deeper into the caverns of her mind. With determination, she threw herself whole-heartedly into her job. If unable to find ease of spirit caused by the heartache of unrequited love, she was at least able to become involved in the complexity of the oil industry, finding it stimulating and absorbing, so that at night, physically and mentally exhausted, she slept untroubled by dreams.

Still outwardly friendly with Blake, she found it difficult not to betray her feelings, especially when she would look up and find him studying her, a perplexed expression on his face, as if he were trying to understand the reason for the subtle change in her.

In an effort to convince herself that she did not love the drilling superintendent, she was seeing a great deal of Peter Corbett. Such evenings were full of fun. Peter constantly avowed his love. Lauren, in turn, refused to take him seriously, and tripped along the romantic edge lightly, unwilling to become drawn into further emotional involvement.

She was aware that events moved swiftly in the oil industry, but even so, she was surprised at the speed with which her own little world changed. Overnight, it seemed, Mr Stewart returned to Akhmar, Blake travelled to England to take up a temporary desk job in the London office, Adele did not renew her contract—but, to Lauren's misery, left for London with a view to purchasing her trousseau. Kath and Ted became engaged and announced their intention to marry in the autumn.

Lauren was delighted with Kath's engagement, but the

prospect of eventually sharing the bungalow with another secretary made her feel depressed. Soon, she told herself, she would have to think about renewing her contract—and next time it would be for a longer period. She enjoyed her job—but did she want to stay in Akhmar? Was it the desert she loved, or was it because of Blake that the desert held such fascination? Would one without the other have any meaning? With innate honesty, Lauren tried to be detached about coming to the right decision, but, with the coming of the summer months, she knew the time had come to make up her mind.

The temperature was beginning to rise and by midday had reached a hundred and ten degrees in the shade. The heat was uncomfortable and employees were reminded to take their daily salt intake, warned that heat exhaustion was not a thing to be taken lightly.

One evening in early June, Lauren accompanied Peter to the formal dance. The chairs and tables arrayed around the pool, the kaleidoscope of moving figures on the dance floor, all served to remind her of her first formal dance. With a tug at her heartstrings, she remembered too easily the figure of Blake as she had seen him standing on the verandah steps. She could recall all too well how he had told her that everything wasn't as simple as it seemed, and that one of the first lessons to learn was to look beneath the surface. She sighed, and wondered if she would ever see Blake again. Bleakly, she surmised he was helping Adele to organise the 'wedding of the year'.

The dance was not proving the pleasurable occasion Lauren had anticipated. When Peter reminded her that he had had to speak to her twice without a reply, she felt guilty and tried her best to become a lively companion, but her efforts met with little success. Eventually, when Peter suggested he take her home, she readily agreed.

As they were about to leave the club, Peter said casually, 'What about taking that trip to Jamil, Lauren?'

'Jamil?' Lauren stared at him blankly.

'Jamil Oasis.' Peter smiled wryly. 'I did promise to take you—don't you remember the lecture I received on how one drives in the desert?' He eyed her speculatively. 'Don't tell me you've forgotten that particular evening?'

Lauren nodded. 'No, I remember it very well. Such a lot's happened since then that Jamil slipped my mind.' She shrugged apologetically. 'Sorry.'

'Forgiven, my love,' Peter assured her without rancour. 'Do you still want to visit Jamil?'

'Yes, I'd love to go,' she said with emphasis. 'I can't afford to miss the chance of seeing a genuine oasis.'

'Let's make it a fortnight tomorrow, then. The temperatures are beginning to climb, so we'd better start early.' Peter shrugged ruefully. 'I can't make it next week—I'm meeting new arrivals.'

'A fortnight tomorrow will suit me fine,' Lauren answered, trying to instill excited anticipation into her reply, but failing.

In silence, they drove to the bungalow. Peter kissed her goodnight, but for once his usual amorous overtures were not prolonged, and she went indoors feeling curiously bereft of emotion.

The next morning, she woke early.

Half-way through the morning, a cable arrived from Blake. Lauren's heart missed a beat as she read the message for a second time. 'Returning Tuesday—14th June. Please arrange transportation—0830 hrs. Airport. Sgd. Elliott.'

As she read the message a third time, its impact hit her. Lauren's heart missed a second beat and then did a triple somersault. Life was suddenly wonderful.

That evening, when Lauren sat down for the ritual of tea-time, Kath said inquisitively, 'What's happened?'

'Nothing,' Lauren shrugged, idly demolishing a sandwich, but she knew Kath was not deceived.

'Come on, Lauren—Give!'

Lauren sipped her tea and said, as if it were of little

interest, 'I did tell you I was going to Jamil with Peter...'

'Yes—and?'

'Blake is coming back next week.' Lauren shrugged nonchalantly. 'I must admit the office has been quiet without him. I've almost forgotten how to make coffee.'

'The office isn't the only thing that's been quiet,' Kath remarked dryly.

Lauren glanced sideways at her friend and saw Kath's face held an uncertain expression. 'What's bothering you, Kath?' she asked, uneasy at the way Kath's usually smooth brow was creased in a frown.

'Lauren ... Do you care for Blake very much?'

'It's difficult not to. Blake Elliott is one of those men that women find irresistible.' Lauren tried to sound sarcastic and failed. 'Why the sudden interest, Kath?'

Kath said quietly, 'Perhaps I've just realised you're in love with him.' She shrugged expressively. 'I've been so busy floating around on my own pink cloud, everything just passed me by.' She stared directly at Lauren. 'I think you ought to know I've heard the rumour that Adele has actually set a date for her wedding. She's getting married in Beirut!'

'To Blake?' Breathlessly Lauren waited for her to reply. It was dreadful to feel one's whole life depended upon a simple answer. She felt like a gambler waiting for the last card to be turned up. Her blood raced, her tongue moistened her lips, and she willed herself to ward off the verbal blow.

'That I don't know, Lauren. Rumours can be so irritatingly vague.' Kath shook her head. 'I just don't understand it. When Adele left here, she made no secret she was going shopping for a trousseau, but when you come to think of it, she never did actually say she was marrying Blake—she just let everyone assume that it was him.' She looked puzzled. 'Now you say Blake is coming back to Akhmar?'

'Yes, that's definite,' Lauren replied, and took another sip of her tea.

Kath stared at her with solemn eyes. 'I keep thinking about that supposed secret engagement, but I just can't accept that Blake would agree to such a thing. It's acting out of character. If there was some reason why he couldn't announce his intentions, he'd expect the woman he loved to understand, and be prepared to be patient.'

'I know,' Lauren said quietly. Her common sense had told her the same thing, but because she loved Blake, her emotions were more deeply involved than Kath's and her perceptions more likely to be distorted. 'We could be guilty of wishful thinking, Kath,' she went on. 'We just don't like the idea of Blake being married to a minx like Adele.'

Kath shrugged in agreement.

Lauren said very slowly and quietly, 'Kath, do you remember that quarrel you had with Ted? Did he ever tell you what he and Adele were talking about that day?'

'I'm not likely to forget that row,' Kath said emphatically. 'He told me they'd been discussing a relative, a cousin, I think.' She paused as if she wanted to remember exactly what Dr Massey had told her. 'Ted said he wasn't interested in Adele, and that he wanted me to be his wife, so I didn't probe.' Her face became a reflective cameo, then she said awkwardly, 'However, Lauren, guessing how you feel about Blake, I thought I ought to tell you I'd heard the rumour.' Her voice trailed. Then, as if coming to the rescue, she exclaimed brightly, 'But as Blake is returning next week, you can ask him.'

'I'll do that,' Lauren exclaimed thoughtfully. 'Anyway, Kath, thanks for your concern.' She flicked an imaginary thread off her dress. 'After all, Blake Elliott isn't the only man in the world,' she said, and knew she was only being self-protective.

Tuesday came at last. Lauren sat at her desk trying to concentrate on a complicated tabulation, but her every sense was alert to the fact that Blake would soon arrive. Relentlessly the clock ticked the minutes away, one by one, making the morning seem endless, then the door opened and a familiar voice said, 'Hello, Lauren. Any coffee?'

'Gallons,' Lauren replied breathlessly, feeling transfixed, as those familiar dark blue eyes held her own.

'Did you have a good trip?' she asked him stiltedly as they were drinking coffee. She felt unable to behave in a natural manner.

'Fairish. A bit bumpy after Beirut.'

Lauren wanted to say, 'How's Adele?' but the words stuck in her throat. Instead she said, 'You're looking well.'

Blake nodded. 'A break from routine is a good thing, but constant paper-work is not for me.'

'You'll have to become familiar with it if you're going to work in London for the rest of your life.'

He looked nonplussed. 'What gave you that idea? I haven't the slightest intention of working in London.' He eyed her intently. 'I thought you knew me better than that. I'm a desert man, through and through.'

Lauren shook her head, then looked up at him. From where she sat, Blake seemed immensely tall, broader than she remembered, yet his face was the same, his eyes held the same compelling expression, the voice the same magnetism.

'How did the Arabic go?' he asked.

'Passed.' Lauren smiled. 'What a relief that was, I can tell you! I couldn't believe it, but kept saying *hum-dil-li-la* again and again to the examiners. I really did mean Thanks be to God.'

'Congratulations.' There was the tiniest pause and when Blake spoke again, his voice was timbred with feeling. 'What about having a celebration? Dine with me on Friday?'

'I'd love to,' Lauren replied, then as her brain registered the fact that Friday was the day she had arranged to go to Jamil with Peter, dismay changed her smile to a frown. 'I'd love to, Blake,' she said, 'but I can't. I've arranged to go to Jamil with Peter.' She shrugged helplessly. 'I did promise more than two weeks ago. Perhaps we could dine another time?'

There was a small silence while Blake looked at her, an odd expression in his eyes, but when he spoke there was no emotion in his voice. 'We can't have you disappointing Mr Corbett.' He shrugged nonchalantly. 'As you say, another time.'

It was difficult to believe that the atmosphere could suddenly be charged with undercurrents of feeling in the short time she had been talking to him, but from the beginning, he had stirred an awareness in her, and they could not meet without some reaction.

She watched him walk to the door. He turned and stared at her, then said tonelessly, 'When you go to Jamil, remember to dress wisely, take plenty of water and start early. The temperatures are climbing.' Then he was gone, and Lauren knew she had not deceived herself at all. She loved Blake Elliott; there was no denying it. Miserably she wiped a tear from the corner of her eye, then, dutifully, she continued her typing.

When Peter had first suggested the visit to Jamil, the thought of seeing a real oasis had brought all sorts of romantic pictures into her mind, making Lauren feel the trip was an opportunity not to be missed. Now, she felt the edge of her anticipation had been dulled by the knowledge that she could have been dining with Blake.

Annoyed with herself that she should let him dominate her thoughts, she concentrated on dressing wisely in cotton shirt and slacks and, clutching a wide-brimmed hat, she waited for Peter to arrive.

The day got off to a bad start when Peter phoned to say he had overslept, and it was after seven-thirty when he finally arrived. They left by the southern route and, after the familiar sights of the oil town were left behind, Lauren settled herself comfortably in the car and looked with interest at the unfolding landscape. In the distance, the escarpment was bathed in a lilac haze threaded with flame, while on either side of the track the desolate wastes were broken only by occasional *sidr* trees, or groups of nomads.

The sun was climbing high in the sky and it began to grow uncomfortable in the confined space of the car. 'Whew! Isn't it hot?' Lauren commented with feeling, and fanned herself with the wide-brimmed hat.

Peter apologised. 'Afraid so, Lauren. That's why I intended leaving earlier. Sorry I overslept.' He glanced sideways at her and smiled encouragement. 'Have patience, princess. We won't be too long before we hit Jamil.'

The longer they drove, the greater became Lauren's need for sight of the oasis. The glare of the sun, the brilliant sky and the endless landscape of sand made her feel drowsy. The temperature rose and she longed for a cool wind to relieve the enervating heat.

The hostility of the dusty terrain that lay on either side of the narrow corrugated track that led to Jamil touched her with a sense of uneasiness. She turned to speak to Peter, but he had both hands firmly on the driving wheel, and watching his now stern profile, she knew it would be unwise to break his concentration. On and on, they continued to drive, the car jerking sporadically over the ridged track. Lauren's eyes ached behind the dark glasses she wore and, when she saw the fringe of palm trees etched against the sky, she felt weak with gratitude.

Peter had also sighted the palm trees. 'There's Jamil,' he exclaimed. 'Isn't it a sight for sore eyes?'

'It certainly is,' Lauren thankfully agreed.

'We'll be there in a jiffy,' he told her. 'Won't I be glad to get into the shade, not to mention enjoying the food and drink!'

Lauren hardly heard him. She felt the world had suddenly grown very still. It was a remarkable thing to come out of the pitiless heat and to see, in between heaven and earth, green blended against golden sand. For the first time in her life, she understood why people talked with reverence in their voices about finding an oasis in the wilderness.

Peter made a direct course for the tress. They set the hamper beneath the palms that fringed the wide pool and, with a sigh of relief, Lauren dipped her handkerchief in the water and enjoyed the luxury of cooling her hands and face, before sitting beside Peter, who was already seated on a cotton rug. Lauren had little appetite, but Peter ate heartily, enjoying the appetising lunch his servant had packed. They drank lager and several cups of coffee.

After they had finished the meal, and the remains of the picnic were cleared away, Peter stretched out lazily, his right arm shading his eyes. Lauren smiled and propping her back against a palm, her arms clasped around her knees, she settled down to relax.

Not a breath of wind stirred the tops of the trees. A lizard lay sprawled on a rock nearby. Yet for all the apparent peacefulness of the scene, there was a solitude about the never-ending waves of drift sand she could see in the distance that filled her with a disquietude for which she could find no answer.

She must have dozed, for she opened her eyes to see Peter now sitting up, staring into the distance. His face seemed withdrawn, and although he had been unusually silent, Lauren had attributed this to fatigue after the concentrated effort required for driving along the desert track. Now she was not sure.

'Is there anything the matter?' she asked, concerned.

He shook his head, then moved towards her. He sat beside her, and reluctantly it seemed, said, 'My contract is up shortly and I'm wondering what to do. Up to now, I've gone where the fancy led me.' He rested his hand on her shoulder. 'Since meeting you, Lauren, I've found myself giving the future a great deal more thought.' He eyed her intently. 'It's about time I settled down.'

Lauren moved uneasily. The last thing she wanted to do was to become involved in a discussion on love and marriage. Casually, she picked up her hat and shook it gingerly in case some adventurous scorpion had crawled inside.

Peter spoke again. 'Thinking about the future is a serious business.'

'I agree,' she said lightly, and put her hand on his arm. 'Perhaps after you've had your leave, seen your family, looked at the wide wicked world again, you might know what you want to do?'

His gaze flickered over her and he remarked cryptically, 'The problem might be *who* I want to do it with.'

'That's always the important part,' Lauren answered, flippantly, feeling a stab of envy that Adele could share her life with Blake. She fanned herself with her hat. It was hotter than she had ever known, and it would not start cooling down for some hours. She was adjusting her hat to give the maximum shade when Peter's fingers tipped it backwards. Gently he stroked the nape of her neck, then, with a swift movement, he turned and cupped her face between his hands. He kissed her, lightly at first, but then the pressure of his firm lips demanded more than she was ready to give.

'Let's not get carried away by the romantic setting,' she said lightly, unwilling to hurt his feelings.

Reluctantly, he let her go. 'You're made for someone to love, Lauren, but somehow I get the idea I'm not that someone.' His gaze was questioning and rather sad.

'I've told you before, Peter,' Lauren said gently. 'I like you, but liking isn't love. It can't be forced.'

'Yes, I know that—now.' The serious note that now charged his voice made her wonder if it was really Peter Corbett speaking. Was this the lad who had an eye for a pretty girl and made no pretence when he flirted outrageously?

'I've made up my mind to be a career woman,' she told him. 'Romance gets one's life too involved.'

Peter shrugged. 'You're right there, princess.' He glanced at his watch. 'Well, the party's over, we'd better make tracks.'

It was mid-afternoon when they left Jamil, and as they

drove towards the outward fringes of the palm trees, the thought of the drive back to the oil town made Lauren feel restless. She longed only for the trip to be over. It had been an uncomfortable journey even in the first exciting hours of the morning, but now she had seen the oasis, the heat of the day had taken its toll, and she didn't look forward to the drive back to Akhmar with joy.

They drove in silence, with Peter once again concentrating on the corrugated track that was their lifeline back to base.

After they had been driving for some time, Lauren again sensed that disquietude that had haunted her all the day long. There seemed to be a profound silence everywhere. It seemed that the bare and stony desert, and every form of life in it, was waiting for something to happen, yet to Lauren, the landscape appeared unchanged. 'Do you feel something in the atmosphere?' she asked her companion. She was croaking now, the sand embracing her throat. The cool drinks at the oasis were a forgotten pleasure.

'No, I don't,' Peter said crossly. 'Stop worrying, Lauren. Settle back, and let me concentrate on the driving.'

Lauren felt jaded, knowing suddenly the day had turned sour.

He must have sensed the change in her. 'Sorry, Lauren,' he apologised. 'I didn't mean to bark.' He sighed. 'It's getting too bumpy for my liking,' he said, and tightened his grip on the wheel as the car bumped and rocked alarmingly. 'I think I'll try that white patch of sand,' he told her, 'it looks firm enough.' With that pronouncement, he swung the car off the track, and there was a sudden juddering as the engine stalled. Peter shook his head with vexation and started the engine again, but when he put the car into gear and released the clutch, the rear wheels spun uselessly and sank deeper into the soft sand.

With a muttered oath, Peter thrust the gear lever into reverse, but again only the screaming noise of the wheels, spinning uselessly in the sand, sounded over the roar of the engine. Slowly the car sank lower at the back, until all they could see was the sky through the windscreen.

Peter groaned. 'Oh, my God! Of all the things to happen!' His fingers clenched the wheel. 'How the hell are we going to move it?'

With a shake of his head, he thrust open the door and climbed out, his feet plodding in the treacherous sand as he went to the rear of the vehicle. Moments later, he trudged back, and said wearily, 'Move over into the driver's seat, Lauren, and take off the brake. When she's in gear, rev hard on the accelerator. Wait till I tell you. Right?'

Lauren nodded and moved behind the wheel. 'Right,' she confirmed.

'Good. Now remember, when I say go, give it all you can.'

'Okay, Peter.' Glancing through the rear screen, she could see him bracing himself against the back of the car.

'Go!' he called. She released the clutch, and pressed hard on the accelerator as he had instructed. But the wheels still spun uselessly. With an exclamation of disgust, Peter called. 'It's no use, Lauren. There's no point in trying again.'

Lauren leaned out of the window and watched him trudging towards her. His face was wet with perspiration. His fair hair hung limply and was plastered with soft sand thrown up by the spinning wheels. Panting, he opened the door and slid in beside her.

'We're stuck,' he told her, and one look at his face made her realise the gravity of that statement.

She knew the dryness in her mouth was caused not only by the heat, but the taste of fear that now tipped her tongue. Now, as she listened to Peter's muttered oaths as he realised they were marooned, the image of Blake and the memory of his voice, searing in its scorn, made Lauren understand, at last, why he was so contemptuous of so-called admin types who professed to know this land in all its tyrannical moods.

She had already seen the arrogance of Blake, had felt anger at his intolerance. Now she had a greater insight into the man, and knew he had to be strong to survive in these primitive conditions; knew that ruthlessness had to be part of his character to enable him to combat the savagery of the desert at its worst.

It was unbearably hot. Lauren felt she would never feel cool again. As far as the eye could see, the burning desert lay brooding under the brilliant sky, hostile and desolate, making her feel she and Peter were the only people left alive in the whole world.

She shook her head impatiently. They had a little food and even less water. Their knowledge of desert survival was slight, but she knew emotion must be kept under tight control. Panic could prove fatal. Trying to think calmly, she said to Peter, 'What will happen when we're missed?'

He shrugged. 'You know everyone leaving Akhmar has to report details of any trips to Transport Department. When a vehicle fails to report in, search procedures are put into operation.' There was an expression on his face that she did not at first understand, then, as comprehension dawned, she said in horrified tones,

'Peter, you did tell Transport?'

Abjectly, he shook his head. 'In the rush of oversleeping, I forgot.' He gave a helpless shrug. 'Whatever we do, Lauren, we must stay with the car—that's the cardinal rule of desert survival. If we try to walk, we'd end up going round in circles. We're told to stay put. That's why the car-roofs are painted white—easier for the helicopter to spot.'

'Thank God, I told Kath,' Lauren said with reverence. 'When we fail to get back, she'll get things moving.'

They sat in silence. Under Peter's sun-tan, his face had a pallor that caused her anxiety. His shirt showed dark patches of sweat after his exertions in trying to move the car. He had tied a handkerchief round his forehead to stop the sweat running into his eyes. She felt sudden compassion for him. She knew, at last, that he had come up against something he could not cope with, and deep inside, he must be tasting the bitter fruit of personal defeat.

The heat clung to her like a second skin from which she could not free herself. Her clothing was uncomfortable and trickles of perspiration gathered in a pool between her breasts, wrinkled her chin and plastered her shirt to her back in uncomfortable rivulets. The desire to breathe cool air was overwhelming.

As time passed, she held Peter's hand. Like two children, lost in the night, they found comfort in each other's presence, not bothering to talk, but husbanding their strength for what they knew could be a long wait.

Finally, with the water practically finished, Peter slept. After a while, he opened his eyes and looked at Lauren, and with a sense of shock, she realised he didn't recognise her. His voice was slurred with delirium. 'I didn't mean to leave you, Tracey. I love you. I've always loved you. I thought I'd forgotten you—but now it's too late. Tracey, oh, Tracey!'

Lauren felt she must be dreaming. It was the heat which was making her delirious, she told herself. Peter and the photograph of Tracey on Blake's desk formed part of a nightmare. It was difficult to keep awake as heat and exhaustion took its toll. As Peter sank into a deep sleep, she began to wonder if death walked in that hostile infinity of sand surrounding them, and inwardly, she wept because she had never been able to tell Blake how much she loved him.

CHAPTER TEN

FURTHER and further, Lauren was drawn into that mystical mood of the desert where fact and fancy meet halfway. She became enmeshed in a web of dreams and thought herself to be hammering on some great door with all her might. Desperately, she prayed that the door would open and she would be taken out of the nightmare which enshrouded her.

The noise altered, and eventually penetrated to her inner senses, making her open her eyes. Blake was rapping on the windscreen. With a great effort, she opened the car door. 'Oh, Blake!' she gasped. 'Thank God, you've found us!' Tears sprang to her eyes and, as his arms held her close, she clung to him for dear life; half afraid that if she let go, he would disappear like a mirage. 'How did you know where we were?' Lauren's lips trembled as she gazed up at Blake as if she had never truly seen him before.

Gently his hands stroked her hair and she felt comfort in the nearness of him. 'Radio has more uses than dancing to,' he told her, and telling her all would be well, he went round to the other side of the car, jerked it open to reveal Peter who was making an attempt to sit up.

Blake's eyes were dark and glittering with fury, and Lauren knew previously she had only witnessed the tip of the iceberg of his anger. He glared at Peter. 'You damned fool, Corbett,' he said quietly. 'Of all the irresponsible fool-hardy people I know, you're at the top of the list.' He gave the younger man a scathing look. 'Why didn't you let Transport know where you were going? You talk to people as if you know the desert backwards, but this isn't like the one you expound to new arrivals. This one hasn't got tarmac roads. You haven't even had the sense to keep on the track—*and* risking Lauren's neck. You bloody fool!'

As if Blake's anger was the last straw to be placed on his back, Peter tried to sit up, his mouth quivering with the effort it was taking him to talk. His voice was harsh with emotion. 'Elliott,' he retorted, 'you can go to hell!' He tried to say more, then collapsed. His eyes were glazed, his face had a sickly pallor. His skin was dry as parchment.

Blake controlled his anger and with a quick movement leaned over him, touching his forehead with expert hands. 'Hell and damnation,' he flared, 'all we want now is for you to go down with heat exhaustion!' Straightening, he said brusquely, 'Lauren, we'll abandon the car. Transport can collect it later, if the Bedouins leave anything.' He looked at her critically. 'Thank God, you're still perspiring. Under these conditions, it's a good sign. Go over to my car and help yourself to a sip of water. Afterwards, open the tailgate of the car. I'll bring Corbett.'

Lauren nodded weakly and followed his instructions. Wretched as she felt, Blake's presence was sufficient to assure her that everything would be all right.

Without apparent effort, Blake picked up Peter and carried him to the car where he laid him on the car floor and started removing his clothing. Seeing Lauren's embarrassment, he said sharply, 'Don't be such a prude, woman. What does clothing matter? If I don't strip him the man will die.' He nodded. 'Get the water from the water-bags slung on the side of the car. Move!'

It was frightening to see Peter, usually so vital, so full of charm, lying there, too exhausted to move. Peter couldn't die! He couldn't. Panic rose to her throat, pushing her voice into a scream, then Blake said calmly, 'Soak handkerchiefs in water and press them around his head. Wipe the inside of his mouth. Keep on doing that until I tell you to stop.'

They worked together as a team, then Lauren heard Blake curse. 'Damn! We're running short of water. I'd better get what's left from your car.'

'There's none left,' Lauren said tonelessly.

Without a flicker of an eyelid, he picked up Peter's jacket. 'I'll take this and soak it in the water from the radiator.'

Watching Blake stride to the abandoned vehicle, she was amazed at his ingenuity and now had no need to wonder why he was so contemptuous of office-wallahs.

He returned quickly and continued with his ministrations. After what seemed an eternity, but was in reality only a short time, he stood up and drew in a deep sigh. 'We've won. He's sweating again, so it's just a matter of getting him—and my desert rose—back to base.' Lauren looked at him quickly, but his expression was impassive. He lit two cigarettes and put one between her lips. 'Draw on that—it will relax you.'

Automatically, she smoked the cigarette, then the full impact of the experience hit her. 'Oh, Blake,' she quavered, 'if you hadn't found us, I don't know what we would have done!'

'Curtains,' came Blake's laconic reply, as he was speeding away, and making radio contact with Transport Department, requesting that they inform the hospital of Peter's condition.

Peter was lying asleep on the rough bed Blake had made for him in the back of the vehicle. Lauren turned and touched his forehead, and as she felt the moisture on his skin, gratitude filled her. She glanced at Blake's firm hands on the wheel, his wrists lean and strong, one circled by the thick band of his watch. How assured he seemed, yet she sensed a tautness about him that made her feel uneasy.

'What's the matter?' she asked apprehensively.

'God! What a day this is turning out to be,' Blake observed. 'A sandstorm is just what the doctor ordered.'

'Sandstorm?'

'That's what I said. You get so you can smell one blowing up before you can see it.'

Shortly afterwards Lauren noticed that there was something different about the horizon. Its thin line seemed to be thickening—a sulphurous mist mingled with the white glare of the sun—causing a curious haziness. Huge yellow spinning tops that she had heard the Arabs called 'dust devils' started to whirl over the surface of the ground at tremendous speed. She felt at any moment that they would stop and some evil spirit would manifest itself. Small saffron clouds were scurrying around the usually clear sky as if trying to escape the attacking currents of air that headed them in all directions. The haze on the horizon changed to a heavy ochre ball of smoke, that rolled towards them, increasing in size as it ate up the sand.

The sky had an unnatural amber look about it, making the day darker than it should have been. The ball of smoke became a ball of fire that turned into a monstrous wave which headed straight for them. The roar of the wind heralded its coming, and Lauren thought the wailing of banshees would sound like a lullaby in comparison, and knew the fury of that noise would echo through dreams that would turn into nightmares.

As the wave of sand covered them, the car seemed to become full of hot wind and flame and sand that bit into Lauren's face like a million enraged insects that captured her in their suffocating embrace. She found it difficult to think or talk. Blake kept firm control of the car and, sensing her fear, he slid his arm around her shoulders.

His touch gave her confidence, and she smiled faintly. 'How can you concentrate on two things at once?' she gasped.

'Which of the two shall I stop?' She thought she heard a mocking tone in his voice as he squeezed her shoulder. 'If you're worried about going off the track again, remember I'm no novice, and although we can only see a few feet ahead, there's only one track and the vibration of the wheels tells me we're still on it. Relax, girl.'

'I will,' she said gratefully. She wanted to say so much more, but the words were lost in fatigue.

'The sandstorm's abating,' he said. 'We've passed through the middle of it, I reckon.'

'How can you tell?'

'If you look to the right, you can see the glow of the gas flares.'

Sure enough, through the haze of the sand, she saw the dull orange glow, and no brighter beacon had ever been more welcome.

His fingers pressed into her shoulders. 'You see, you can rely on Uncle Blake. He always knows where he is.'

'Has there ever been a time when you didn't know where you were?' Lauren couldn't resist asking, feeling light-hearted now the danger was over.

'Only with a certain redhead,' was his unexpected retort.

'One needs to persevere with redheads,' she reminded him, 'so I wouldn't give up hope.'

'I won't.'

She glanced at him and, as he turned, she saw a glint of amusement in the blue eyes. That was the final straw. In that moment, she wanted to do so many things. She wanted to weep because they were near home. She wanted to laugh with joy because Peter was safe. She wanted to fling her arms around Blake's neck, and kiss him and tell him she loved him. Instead she said quietly, 'I'm glad.'

The events of the day were making her lightheaded, she suspected and, not to get further into deep water, she looked at the landscape again. In the distance she saw a tree, that, until a few minutes ago, had been an indistinct shadow.

'You were right,' she said. 'It's clearing.'

Blake smiled indulgently. 'Now you can see the escarpment.'

The light from the air rushed to meet them, the sky above widened and suddenly there was freshness like a balm on their sand-soaked skins. It was difficult to believe that the sandstorm had only lasted one hour. Driving through it had seemed a lifetime.

Peter was now awake but, apart from giving Lauren a weak smile, he lay without movement.

Soon they were at the hospital entrance. Blake organised a stretcher and helped Peter out of the car.

The bungalow seemed more like home than ever. Awkwardly, Lauren stood beside Blake. He seemed to sense what she intended to say and stopped her by placing the tips of his fingers on her lips. 'Don't try to thank me, Lauren,' he said. 'I'm glad I was the one to get to you in time.' He scanned her face intently. 'Come on, you've had a rough day. Best thing is to take a quick shower, then sleep some. I'll see you in the morning.'

Lauren gripped his arm tightly. She knew the moment had come to ask him about Adele, but after the last few hours, she couldn't stand the uncertainty. Her throat was parched. The aftermath of the sandstorm was not altogether responsible, for she experienced inner tension as her own feelings reached flashpoint.

'Blake,' she said hesitantly, 'I've heard a rumour that Adele has set a date for her wedding.' Her voice trailed and she could not continue. Looking up at him, she surprised a strange expression on his face, but he answered her readily enough.

'Yes, Lauren. Adele is getting married—in Beirut.'

Lauren gave a sharp intake of breath and, as if deciding she had suffered enough for one day, Blake put his hands on her shoulders and said softly, 'But she's not marrying me.'

Lauren thought the day had been so full of emotion, she could contain no more, but Blake's news about Adele filled her with elation which was so strong that it flooded out every other feeling.

Very gently he bent his head and kissed her. 'Now, do as I tell you, woman—go indoors and rest.'

Lauren soon recovered from her ordeal. Blake was amiable, and Mr Stewart's concern for his secretary's welfare was heartwarming to her.

After forty-eight hours, Peter was discharged from the hospital. He telephoned Lauren to apologise for being such a fool. He said he was feeling much better and added, with a trace of belligerence in his voice, that he intended to visit the main office later that day in order to see Blake. Lauren sensed the showdown was on the way.

Mr Stewart, the director, was accompanying the general manager who had arranged to visit local dignitaries. Blake was dealing with schedules when Peter arrived. Lauren had never seen Peter in such a mood before. Although he was pale beneath his tan, he held his shoulders erect, and she sensed he did not intend to be deterred.

As she opened the door for him to enter the director's office, the atmosphere was chilly. Watching Blake and Peter face each other, Lauren knew the moment of truth had come.

When Blake spoke, his voice was clipped. 'Well, Corbett,' he said. 'After all, you were told about climatic conditions—and after I personally pointed out to you the hazards of the terrain, you still went on in your own reckless fashion. You behaved in a totally irresponsible manner, not only endangering your own life, but putting Miss Fletcher at risk. You're a menace, Corbett. You always have been, and always will be.'

'Elliott,' Peter said jerkily. 'First, let me thank you for saving my life, and secondly, let me tell you to go to hell!' He clenched his fists. 'God, how I've rued the day you crossed my path!'

'I'd gladly go to Hades, just for the pleasure of seeing you there, Corbett.' There was a touch of grim humour in his voice. 'Damn you! When I think of you endangering Miss Fletcher's life—and when I think of what you did to Tracey, I could slaughter you, willingly!'

Peter stood immovable. 'As far as Lauren's concerned, a man couldn't find a better or more loyal companion. As for Tracey—I'm going to marry her, if she'll still have me.' He thrust his face towards Blake, aggressively. 'I'm determined to see her, whatever you do, so I'll take my chance on living after you've done with me.'

Blake's face became set, but the dark eyes glinted. 'Keep away from her,' he warned.

'That depends on Tracey herself.' There was a wall of silence. Peter tried again, his tone changing from one of defiance to reason. 'Believe me, Blake, when I first met Tracey, I felt sorry for her. I didn't know anyone could be that naïve—I tried to show her the lighter side of life, give her some fun, but she took my attentions too seriously, and before I knew it, she told me she'd fallen head over heels in love with me.' Peter drew in a long slow breath. 'I felt trapped by what I thought was her possessiveness. I didn't realise then that it was her reaction to Monica's treatment, that she isn't at all possessive.' He shook his head. 'Later, as I came to know her better and realised how Monica hated her, the situation was out of control.' He put one hand on the desk as if to steady himself.

Blake lit a cigarette and crumpled the empty packet into a tight ball. 'Go on,' he said.

Peter shrugged. 'Bad luck your old man had to get mixed up with Monica.' He looked at Blake's impassive figure. 'Couldn't have delighted you to have my dear aunt for a stepmother. It was only when I stayed with them that I realised how Monica hated her own daughter.' His lips twisted wryly. 'I knew she'd always been the vain one of the family, but when her daughter started to steal the lime-light—God, how cruel she was!' He scowled at Blake. 'But you weren't there to see Monica blow the whole thing out of proportion. You weren't there to see anything—you were in your damned desert!' His voice rose angrily. 'You came in at the end to pick up the pieces, to hear Monica's version of how her no-good nephew had driven Tracey to a breakdown by his false declarations of love. You believed everything she told you.' The last sentence was an accusation.

'I believed the evidence of my own eyes,' Blake said quietly, and drew on his cigarette. He paused, blew out a thin stream of smoke. 'When I left Tracey, she was a lovely young girl. When I saw her again, she was a nervous wreck, all her illusions destroyed. When I saw the most trusting creature I ever knew suddenly become distrustful of everyone, I hated your guts.'

As Lauren stood witness to the scene, gripped by the drama that was being enacted before her eyes, she felt unable to move as the strong currents of their antagonism and emotion washed over her, holding her captive.

Blake spoke again, but his voice was so low it was as if he were speaking to himself. 'When Father married Monica and she insisted he return to England, I hated her for that alone. She destroyed him, took him away from the only life he loved so she could be near the bright lights of London. The only compensation of that marriage was Tracey. When I returned to Guildford and saw the wreck you'd made of Tracey's life and saw my father turn into an old man before he died, I would have gladly broken your neck.'

'Breaking my neck might have been the kindest thing.' Peter shrugged. 'I've suffered for that mistake.' His eyes rested glitteringly on Blake's averted face. 'Now let me give you the laugh of your life, because the tables were well and truly turned on this handsome golden boy. After I got away from the whole damned mess, I found I cared for Tracey. After so many affairs with women who would never be faithful, I thought it was a reaction that would fade.' His voice lowered dramatically. 'Then, stranded in the desert and thinking I was going to die, I knew I loved Tracey and I'd let a gem slip through my fingers.' His face became set. 'Now, laugh your fill, and do your damnedest! My contract finishes next month, then I'm returning to England to ask Tracey to marry me. I only hope I'm not too late.'

Peter's face was now devoid of colour. His voice trailed away, his arms hung limply to his sides. He shook himself as if he could not believe he had actually stood up to Blake Elliott, had said the things he had said, had made the decision to marry Tracey Elliott.

Tracey—The photograph on Blake's desk, Peter's words at the oasis, were now explained. Lauren's heart was racing. How would Blake react? His silence seemed interminable, then he crushed his cigarette into the ashtray with deliberation.

'At least the desert seems to have made a man of you, Corbett,' he said patronisingly, 'but, by all that's holy, if you ever cause Tracey further unhappiness, you'll wish you'd never been born.' He shrugged, almost helplessly. 'If she still wants to marry you, I can't stop her, but you'd better be quite sure you know what you're doing.' He stared at Peter with narrowed eyes. 'Otherwise, look out—you'll have me to deal with!'

. Blake looked up, and a startled expression appeared in his eyes as he saw Lauren standing at the door. He seemed only now to be aware of her presence. He drew his brows together in a frown. 'Sorry you had to hear all that. Not very thoughtful of us.' He looked at Peter and there was a wealth of meaning in his expression. 'I hope you haven't been hurt too much, Lauren.'

'It's all right, Blake,' Lauren answered. Her voice was the barest murmur. 'I'm not in love with Peter, if that's what you mean. Peter's never been in love with me. We both know it's an emotion that can't be forced. We're fond of each other.' She turned to face Peter. 'I hope things turn out the way you want them.'

With a ghost of a smile that resembled the old Peter, he said more cheerfully, 'I'll let you both know,' then he walked out of the office.

'Did you mean it when you said you didn't love Peter, or was that just to save your pride?' Blake's voice was casual.

Lauren said simply, 'Every word I spoke was the truth.'

He moved towards her and tilted her chin. 'Sometimes I don't think you know anything about love at all, Lauren. It isn't the wonderful thing you think it is. It can change people.' There was a bitterness about his mouth and Lauren sensed he was thinking of his father.

She sighed. The desert claimed Blake, and he didn't intend to repeat his father's mistake.

She put her hand up to touch his. 'You're wrong, Blake. I know a lot about love. You're the one who has the whole thing out of perspective.' Sadly she returned to her office, glad at least to feel the familiarity of the typewriter keys clicking beneath her fingers.

A week passed and she neither saw nor heard from Blake, then one morning he arrived in the office and laid a sheaf of papers on her desk. 'That lot will keep you out of mischief while I'm in Beirut.'

'Beirut?' she queried.

'Yes.' Blake smiled and Lauren was dismayed to see the old mockery in his eyes.

Picking up the reports he had given her for typing, she asked casually, 'How long will you be away?'

'About a week. The reports are straightforward. If there's any difficult technical term you can't understand, ask Mr Stewart.'

'When are you leaving?'

'On this afternoon's plane.'

Lauren felt like shaking him. His laconic replies infuriated her, yet she had to admit there was no reason why he should inform her of his plans.

After Blake had gone, she felt a pang of envy—or was it more a case of wishful thinking?

While Blake was away in Beirut, Peter telephoned to say he had heard from Tracey and was leaving Akhmar. Before ringing off, he said he would like to take Lauren out to dine the evening before he left.

During dinner, Peter kept the conversation flowing in a lighthearted vein, yet the man who looked at Lauren across the table was a different person from the one who had introduced her to champagne cocktails only a few months earlier. The carefree boyish look had gone, but the new maturity in his face made him more attractive than before. Lauren knew, inevitably, that women would be drawn towards him. She hoped Tracey would instinctively understand such things, and they would find happiness together.

'I'm glad Tracey has agreed to see you, Peter,' she told him. 'I knew if she loved you, she couldn't help herself.'

'I hurt her so much, Lauren.' He shook his head. 'It's only the events of the past few weeks that have made me realise how much. I was never so perceptive before—or so vulnerable. I tried to talk to you about it at the oasis. The future, I said.'

'Bright with promise, I hope.'

'You're a brick, Lauren. After my vows of undying love for you, it would have served me right to have the sharp edge of your tongue.' He grinned impishly. 'Instead of which, here you are acting the part of my guardian angel.'

'I knew your vows of undying love weren't for real,' Lauren said smilingly. 'You flirted so outrageously, I took everything you said with an oceanful of salt.'

'Wise girl.' Peter placed a hand over hers. 'Some guy is going to be lucky one day. I hope he realises how fortunate he is.' He added cryptically, 'The one thing I've never taken Blake Elliott for is a fool. I'm not going to start thinking he is one now.'

When the time came to say goodnight and goodbye, he held her gently and kissed her on the lips. 'I'll never forget you, Lauren.' He pushed a small packet into her hands. 'I'd like you to have this as a souvenir. I think you're . . .' He stopped, at a loss for words.

'I know, Peter,' she said for him. 'Friendship is love without its wings.'

'That says it all, Lauren. Goodnight, Princess, and goodbye.'

Lauren watched the car drive away, happy that Peter had found out what really mattered to him. She prayed that Tracey would marry him, and not be afraid to take a second chance.

In a mixed mood, she switched the lights on in the lounge and drifted to the settee. She sat down, thinking over the turn of events, then remembered the package. She opened it to find that it contained a box which held a necklet of gold squares. Upon each square an Arabic symbol had been inscribed. It was beautiful.

Blake returned from Beirut in time to attend Kath's farewell party. It was a small, intimate affair. Kath was popular and everyone was pleased about the wedding.

While Alan ribbed Ted unmercifully about joining the ranks of the married men when he went back to England in September, Molly was unashamedly romantic and talked about orange-blossom and the joys of marriage.

Kath grinned. 'That's one day my three beautiful sisters will have to take a back seat,' she said happily.

'That's a sentiment I heartily endorse,' Lauren told her.

A toast was drunk to Kath's future with Ted, and then Blake surprised everyone by saying he had an announcement to make. 'This seems an appropriate moment to tell you that Sister Adele Harding has become engaged to my very good friend, Dr John Frost. They're to marry shortly, and intend living in the United States.'

The chatter of voices asking Blake innumerable questions seemed to be coming from a long way off. Lauren's heart twisted with joy. Adele was going to marry John Frost. No wonder some of her earlier remarks had been the cause of Blake's perplexity!

As the evening drew to a close, Blake touched Lauren's arm. 'Let's go on the verandah for a breath of fresh air,' he suggested, and Lauren agreed.

It was a beautiful night and the moonlight shed a soft radiance everywhere, silhouetting the tamarisk trees against the velvet sky. Blake put his arm around her shoulder. It was so easy to become susceptible to his charms, so difficult to be casual, that she said coolly, 'Your announcement made quite a stir in there. More than one person expected you to marry Adele.' Then, suddenly daring, she rushed on, 'Are you dreadfully upset that she's marrying someone else?'

Blake smiled sardonically. 'You're taking it for granted I was in love with Adele, and therefore I must be heart-broken.' He eyed her quizzically. 'You certainly did jump the gun thinking that we were planning marriage.' He looked hard at Lauren and she felt herself mesmerised by his stare. 'I'd never marry a woman I didn't love,' he told her. 'I admire Adele. She's efficient, never panics, and she puts her cards on the table—before marriage, not after-wards.' Lauren knew he was thinking of Monica, but she said nothing. With a teasing gesture, he ruffled her hair. 'Admiration isn't love. Surely you know that, if nothing else.' He shrugged expressively. 'Besides, any woman I love has to go my way. Adele's used to people following her.'

'I'm glad you don't love her,' Lauren said, then not want-ing to sound brazen, she added, 'I wouldn't like you to have been hurt by Adele falling in love with someone else.'

'There's one thing you might like to know, and that is why I gave the impression that Adele and I were—shall we say—interested in each other.'

Lauren nodded. 'Yes, I'd like to know what lay behind that masquerade.'

'John Frost and I became good friends after that accident I had in El Rubai,' Blake went on. 'When he and Adele decided to think about marrying, John asked if I would keep an eye on her. After all, Adele is a beautiful woman, and out here, with men outnumbering women, she would have been under constant pressure to go out with them. As everyone thought she was the girl-friend of the drilling superintendent, they didn't pester her for dates. Simple as that.'

'Yes, a lot of things are easy to understand when they're explained.' Lauren knew her smile was too bright. 'And no one got hurt, so everyone lives happily ever after.' She moved towards the door, and as the light passed over

Blake's face, his expression was inscrutable and once more he was the man of complexity she had encountered when she had first arrived in Akhmar.

After the party was over, Kath tapped on her door. 'Lauren, can I come in? I'm too excited to sleep. Can we talk? I've got something to tell you.'

Lauren smiled at the excitement in Kath's voice. 'Come in, poppet,' she called.

Kath padded in and sat beside Lauren on the edge of the bed. Her usually placid face now had a greater depth, a serenity of mind and spirit, and to Lauren she epitomised happiness.

'What great secret have you got to tell me?' Lauren asked her.

'Well, the other day you asked me if Ted had told me why he and Adele were constantly in conversation. Later, he told me he and Adele had been talking about a relative.'

'I remember—a cousin, you said.'

Kath nodded. 'Since Blake has announced that Adele and Dr Frost are now engaged, Ted tells me that John Frost is his cousin. Adele apparently met him in Beirut and he fell head over heels in love with her. Surprisingly, Adele seemed similarly attracted. However, when it came to agreeing to marriage, she became cagey. Ted says John is a specialist in the field of tropical medicine and had been offered a super job in the States. Adele, however, insisted he accept the position before she agreed to their engagement. This put John in a difficult situation. He loves Adele, yet he also loves his work in the Middle East. He didn't want to go to the States, but Adele was adamant. Ted was furious that she should be so selfish and said it proved she wasn't really in love with his cousin at all, that she only wanted to be the wife of an influential medical man in the US.' Kath shrugged expressively. 'That's what he was telling her when I bumped into them.' She smiled wistfully. 'Anyway, Lauren, as you heard, they're getting married next month and are going to America later in the year.'

She looked aggressive. 'Oh, Lauren, what a wretch that woman is! I wouldn't care if Ted had to work in Maheil and we had to live in one of those *serifas*. Anywhere with Ted would be heaven.' Her eyes took on a faraway look and Lauren knew Kath meant what she said. She would never be able to understand that Adele was a realist. Furthermore, she would let people know it, before she ensnared them. Adele had her own code.

Lauren recalled Blake's words that any woman he married would have to be prepared to tread any path he chose, even if they were far distant. She felt sorry for Dr Frost. He must love Adele very much indeed to change his life for her. Love made one a prisoner, she thought, and yet if one did love with the intensity needed to make such a sacrifice, one wouldn't think oneself a prisoner. She shrugged sleepily. Her thinking was becoming contradictory.

Kath was almost asleep, and Lauren shook her gently. 'Enough talking for one night,' she told her. 'We'd better get some sleep.' She smiled happily at Kath. 'You're going to need all your energy to go shopping for your trousseau.'

Kath pecked her cheek. 'Gosh, Lauren, I never knew anyone could be so happy! Goodnight.'

Love made one so vulnerable, Lauren thought as her friend left. The great Blake Elliott would never allow himself to be that—so love was something he had banished. His world contained only one thing that made demands on him—*oil*.

How could she hope to compete with that!

CHAPTER ELEVEN

WITH the coming of summer, social life lessened considerably. After exhausting days spent in temperatures rising to a hundred and twenty degrees at noonday, most people preferred to stay indoors. If they did seek relaxation outside, the swimming pool was their favourite venue.

Since Kath's farewell party, Lauren had seen little of Blake. All she knew was that he was kept busy supervising the completion of the rogue well at Number Five. On the odd occasions she met him, there was a brooding quality about him that made her wonder if he loved Adele, after all, and only now was discovering his true feelings.

She sighed and settled to check the complicated reports she had prepared. So intent was she on the job, she did not notice Blake until he stood before her.

'Hullo, Lauren.' He smiled in the way she knew only too well, and she shivered in the air-conditioned room. Blake noticed and laughed. 'You'll soon be a veteran and can boast you've survived a summer,' he told her.

'I'll wait until the end of September before I make such a foolhardy statement.'

'Naturally—but it isn't like you to be so cautious.' As if suddenly impatient with the conversation, he thrust a cablegram into her hand. 'Read this,' he commanded, and silently she took the slip of paper.

'Peter and I were married this morning—by special licence.

Be happy for me, Blake. Love Tracey.'

Lauren whisked a tear from the corner of her eye and hoped Blake wouldn't notice. 'I hope they'll be very happy,' she said earnestly. 'I'm so glad for their sakes that things have turned out this way.'

'Good!' The sound of Blake's voice belied his words. For some reason, Lauren felt the need to reassure him. Was it because he cared for Tracey—or she cared for Blake?

'Peter will make Tracey happy,' she declared fervently. 'I know he will. Even if you still think of him as a playboy—under that surface charm of his, there's so much good in him.'

Blake was obviously unconvinced. 'Glad you think so, Lauren. To hear you talk, you make Peter sound like a knight in shining armour. He should have been christened Sir Galahad.'

Lauren crushed down her anger. 'That's unfair, Blake,' she retorted coolly. 'And you know it.' She handed him back the cablegram. 'I presume you've sent your congratulations?'

'Of course!' His lips tightened, and Lauren realised once again he had misinterpreted her words. Didn't he understand that, whatever else she thought of him, she would never accuse him of petty-mindedness?

Watching him, she recognised that, underneath his harsh façade, he was genuinely concerned about Tracey's happiness.

Aware of her scrutiny, Blake laughed without amusement. 'It would seem, Lauren, that engagements and marriages are in the air. Hassan has invited us to a cousin's wedding.'

'Us?' Lauren queried, raising surprised eyebrows.

'Hassan did tell you he would invite you to an occasion to remember.' He smiled infuriatingly. 'And when I returned the bracelet I told him I intended to marry you. The Sheikh Al Ben Abdul Hassan still thinks we're engaged, so he will expect you to accompany me.'

Blake's arrogant acceptance that she would accompany him made her angry. Her green eyes flashed, but when she spoke there was little expression in her voice. 'I see!' she said, and surprised a reminiscent smile on his face.

With a dreadful nostalgia, she remembered the touch of

his firm lips, and she wished he would not keep stating he intended to marry her. The mockery of it turned a knife in her heart. Brushing aside such thoughts, she asked with feminine logic, 'What do I wear?' She shrugged. 'After all, Arab weddings aren't my usual scene.'

Blake ignored the sarcasm in her voice. When he answered her, it was as if he were explaining some difficult point of etiquette to a somewhat unintelligent guest. 'The important thing is to have arms and shoulders covered. Arabs tend to think Western women are somewhat immoral, and scanty clothing wouldn't improve their opinions.' He raised his eyebrows in sardonic amusement. 'They have feudal ideas about their own womenfolk.'

'Some Westerners have the same ideas,' Lauren pointed out. Unfortunately, she was glancing at the cable from Tracey and, as Blake's lips tightened, she knew he had taken her remark as a personal affront.

She shrugged. 'As you say, weddings are in the air. I'll choose a suitable dress. It should be an interesting occasion.' Despite herself, she leaned towards him and added, 'I've read a lot about Arab weddings.'

Blake said evenly. 'Then, no doubt, you'll know that the bridegroom stands no nonsense and expects complete obedience from his bride. She, in turn, has been trained to accept such an attitude without question.' He looked at Lauren impassively, although she fancied amusement had found a hiding place in the deep-set eyes. 'It's a custom I sometimes think should be encouraged in the Western world.'

'No doubt you do,' Lauren retorted with asperity. 'Men like you don't want to believe women can get along without masculine support.' Her heart was hammering. She realised that he was succeeding in agitating her once again. 'Let me tell you, Blake Elliott,' she continued undeterred, 'that the suffragettes fought for more than the vote and I, for one, don't intend to let any man dictate to me.'

'You sure rate yourself high, Lauren. Any man would be crazy to tie himself up with a bombshell like you. He'd never know when it was going to blow up in his face, so you needn't worry about matrimonial bondage.' His grin was taunting. 'I told Hassan I intended to marry you, but I didn't say when!' He eyed her obliquely. 'Perhaps in a few years, after you've blazed the trail as a career girl, you might find yourself glad to free yourself of those chains of emancipation.'

Lauren remained where she was, gazing at the closed door for several seconds after Blake had departed. The torrent of words that had poured so readily from her lips had not only increased her anger, but had also used up precious energy. In a climate such as Akhmar, such waste could lead to problems.

Blake Elliott had a ruthless streak in him, and wouldn't hesitate to make her toe the line if the game turned out to be one not to his liking. Lauren shrugged impatiently. She had no intention of becoming constantly embroiled in the emotional conflicts which dominated their meetings, so, with a wry smile, she told herself she had better reach a decision about asking for a transfer.

Two days before the Arab wedding, Blake telephoned her to remind her of the arrangements. He ended on the cheerful note that Hassan would introduce her to some Arab ladies who would take her to the bridal reception. Blake would join a 'men only' gathering which was to be held several miles distant.

'Charming,' Lauren replied. 'I thought I was to accompany you to the wedding, not attend solo.'

Blake laughed down the wires. 'It's not my wedding,' he told her. 'My advice is—when in Arabia, do as the Arabs do!'

Listening to the deep resonant tones that had fascinated her from the first, she knew she would not leave Akhmar. As long as she was able to see Blake, everyone else would remain a shadow.

She replaced the receiver, realising as she did so that she was nursing the fond hope that the occasion of the Arab wedding might rekindle that spark of affinity she and Blake had shared at Christmas time—when they had walked along the waterfront, and had gone shopping in the old city of Quamat. Since he had told her that he was past the stage where women could hurt him, Lauren felt something had disappeared from their relationship.

The day of the wedding greeted her with its golden blaze. Excitedly, she dressed with care in the multi-coloured silk dress she had decided to wear for the important day. She looked at herself in the mirror, carefully checked her appearance, and pushed away the vague thoughts of disquietude that filled her. She was thrilled at the prospect of taking a glimpse at one of the close family occasions much loved by the Eastern races, but she felt bewildered that she should be feeling such acute shyness. She chided herself impatiently. Obviously, it was the thought of Blake leaving her alone with the womenfolk!—that, and the fact that her Arabic wasn't that fluent, she reflected wryly.

When Blake saw her, he whistled appreciatively. 'I wish I was keeping you company instead of spending the day with the men,' he told her, and Lauren glowed with satisfaction at this compliment.

'I rather wish the same thing myself,' she replied, noticing the way in which Blake wore the light tropical suit, which only served to accentuate his dark attractiveness.

He took her hands and there was a glint in his eyes as he bent and kissed her cheek. 'Mmm! You smell delightful,' he drawled 'Sandalwood! Fragrant and unforgettable—like the girl who's wearing it.'

Lauren smiled up at him, her eyes bright and provocative. 'I think that's the most chivalrous thing you've ever said to me. Beneath that armour of ice, can there really be a Prince Charming, after all?'

'Perhaps after the wedding, I might show you how well fire and ice can live together.' The mocking note in his voice made her blush furiously. He had used just the right blend of ambiguity to make her think not only of the Arab wedding, but to also remember that he had told Hassan he intended to marry her.

Blake grinned at her, amused at her discomposure. 'Talking about Prince Charming automatically brings Cinderella into the story—and her coach.' He pointed to his new white Pontiac. 'I can't promise to have you home by midnight—life might become too exciting.' She saw amusement in his eyes as he added, 'But I can promise that I won't leave the ball without you.'

Lauren smiled up at him and said puckishly, 'Leave the belle of the ball?—that would never do!' and with a shake of auburn hair, she tripped ahead of him and settled herself comfortably in the passenger seat.

They had just cleared the outskirts of the oil town when a huge black cloud appeared on the horizon. Blake gave a muttered curse and, with a deft movement, swung the car off the roadway on to a desert track. The radio crackled into life, and Mr Stewart's voice filled their ears.

From the intense concentration on Blake's face, Lauren sensed an emergency had arisen, and the words now being spoken by Mr Stewart were beginning to make sense.

'Emergency! Blow-out at Rig Five.

Following action supplemented.

Pipeline department ordered to get all crews to site.

Personnel from adjacent rigs to cease drilling and converge on Rig Five.

Fire and ambulance services alerted.

Transport to send out heavy winch trucks and other vehicles.

Service department to supply all available water-carriers.

Utilities to send out as many men as can be spared.

Move! Keep me informed. Over and out.'

'Okay, Ed, I'm on my way,' Blake replied, and with a quick sideways glance at Lauren, he apologised briefly, 'Sorry, no wedding today. No time to take you back to Akhmar, either.'

All the time Blake had been talking, he was manoeuvring the Pontiac, and before Lauren had time to realise fully what was happening, he was speeding across the desert.

As they raced across the barren land, Lauren's mind seemed to divide itself into two parts. One part was filled with alarm as she recalled Molly Kennedy's words that Blake had been almost killed at El Rubai when a similar emergency had arisen. The other part was conscious of what appeared to be the reckless speed at which Blake was driving the car. With a tremendous effort of will-power, she made logic take over from emotion. This was no time to succumb to personal feelings. Even when the tyres hit a small rut and the car virtually leapt into the air before coming back to land on its four wheels, she said nothing, but made herself concentrate on Blake's strong hands which were holding the steering wheel firmly.

On either side of the thin snaking track lay the bare and stony desert. Its vast expanse was a hostile desolation shimmering in the morning haze. The damned desert, Peter had called it, and perhaps after all he was right. It was certainly no green virgin land, but hot calcined earth that mocked man's efforts to conquer it.

Perspiration was beading Lauren's upper lip and impatiently she brushed it away with the back of her hand. The car seat felt as if it were burning her, making her clothing become moulded to her figure. Even in so short a time, the elegant creature that had left the bungalow no longer existed. In her place there sat a girl whose head ached, whose throat was parched, and who felt shrouded in sand. The thought made her tense and she clenched her fingers about her handbag to help her remain composed.

Blake seemed unaware of any discomfort, and Lauren glanced at his stern profile. His expression was the same as when he had rescued Peter and herself. It was an expression which declared a dedication and concentration to the world of oil and its hazards, which nothing would be allowed to deter. Instinctively Lauren sensed he was gathering all his resources as he mentally tackled the emergency that confronted him at Rig Five.

The treacherous sand surrounding them seemed to undulate and dance before her eyes. White with glare, and frenzied with heat, it moved like the swishing of silk, making Lauren feel sick. Nausea twisted in her stomach as if it sought some outward channel to freedom. She longed for the throbbing at her temple to cease, the lassitude to vanish, and to discover that this devilish ride over rough desert with bumps and clouds of dust was but a dream. By a superhuman effort, she kept the sickness at bay.

The sky was filled with a black pall of smoke that billowed and swirled and almost blotted out the sun itself.

Without warning, Blake swung the car in an easterly direction and the sudden lurching left Lauren breathless. It was now possible to see the rig still standing and, in fascination, she watched the oil push its way into the sky, forming a distinct vee-shape as it eddied upwards.

'It's uncanny seeing the oil form that shape,' Lauren said uneasily. 'It reminds me of a djinn. It makes me believe all the tales I've heard about the spirits of the desert.'

Blake grunted. 'The oil's hitting the crown block of the derrick and being diffused. No magic about it.'

Like a magnet, Lauren's gaze was drawn again to the dark discolouration of the sky where the pent-up oil was soaring hundreds of feet up into the air, joining in unison with the pall of black smoke. Despite the heat, the sight made her shiver. Fire alone was a terrible enemy. Now, allied with the desert, it made a formidable foe.

In the instinctive way he had, Blake once more divined Lauren's thoughts. He said comfortingly, 'Don't worry. Oil men learn the art of survival early.'

They were still some distance from the actual well fire itself when the derrick appeared to sway, then crumple and slowly fall.

Blake muttered, 'Thank God she's gone! At least that's one problem out of the way.'

Lauren stared aghast. 'But what if the rig's fallen on someone? Surely they'd be killed?'

'I reckon—but Mac, my toolpusher, is too good an oil man not to get the men to a distance where they would be safe from the danger of a toppling rig. With the ferocious heat coming from that fire, he'd know that rig would just have to collapse. I hope!'

As they approached nearer the inferno, there was the sound of a heavy drumming on the roof of the car. Black streaks ridged the white paintwork like a woman's mascara streaked by rain. With a muttered oath, Blake switched on the windscreen wipers. At the same time, Lauren noticed that an almost perfect black circle appeared to be forming around the well, and with astonishment, she realised for the first time since she had been in Akhmar that she was seeing the 'real thing'.

'Crude oil,' she gasped. 'So that's what it looks like. I always imagined it to be like thick black treacle.'

'Not so, Lauren,' Blake told her. 'Crude is quite thin.'

He shrugged. 'It's amazing how one can spend a lifetime on an oil location and never see crude. That oil you're seeing now is the fall-out from the unburnt crude at the top of the fire. Because of the tremendous pressure now that the well is flowing free, it's not possible for the fire to consume all the oil. Now that the rig has gone, I would say that the column of fire and oil is over two hundred feet high.'

'It's a sight I'll never forget,' Lauren whispered in awe. Not only the sight, she thought, but the smells. Apart from a sickly cloying smell, mingled with sulphur, that assailed the nostrils, there was the smell of sweat, the smell of sand.

Sand, she thought grimly. Sand that stretched in an endless sea of pitiless white-gold waves, and they were like a small lifeboat going towards a burning tanker, but instead of an ocean, they had to cross that dreadful sea that was a confusion of dunes and troughs that continuously moved.

Now they were nearing the well-head, it was possible to see figures moving about the area. From Blake's tight-lipped expression, Lauren knew he was wondering what carnage lay ahead.

Blake monoeuvred skilfully and, with that economy of movement she had seen previously displayed when he was reviving Peter, he brought the car to a halt by the unit trailer and roughly thrust open the car door and got out.

'*Stay put in the trailer,*' he ordered and, leaving her, he headed swiftly towards a group of men. He was gone before Lauren had the chance to adjust to the fact that the nightmare drive was over and they had arrived.

She got out of the car and stood blinking like an owl awakened in bright sunlight. An almost unbearable heat met her, and she felt she had been thrown into a furnace that served as the entrance to hell where victims were literally burned alive. She could feel an intense pain in her head, and she covered her ears with her hands in an effort to find ease. Only after seconds had elapsed did she realise that the pain was caused by the terrific noise which had been created by the release of pressures unleashed from the depths of the earth and now running rampant with triumphant victory.

The scene was one of intense activity. Vehicles seemed to be arriving from all directions, disgorging the men alerted by the director of oil operations.

Looking at the colour and movement about her, Lauren likened it to one of those kaleidoscopes which, when shaken, formed innumerable patterns.

Everyone was covered in great splashes of the black rain. The circle of oil around the rig was now a pool. There was a sound like thunder, which was the noise of the oil. It was still gushing upwards towards the sky as if to gain its freedom from the earth that had so long kept it imprisoned.

Bewildered, she looked around to see if she could spot Blake. Where was he? A sudden explosion rent the air and caused her to panic. Ignoring the heat, the noise, the fact that by now she was drenched in crude oil, she stumbled in the direction he had taken. Unaccustomed to walking on the soft sand, Lauren's feet sank into the soft surface. Her legs ached with the effort needed to cover only a short distance. The hot air burnt her throat, making her cough and feel sick.

The air reeked with the stench of burning oil, and the roar of the fire made a terrible noise and tortured her ears with a tremendous din. Panic threatened to overcome her, but she thrust the emotion away and knew, whatever discomfort had to be endured, endure it she must, for there would be no peace for her until she reached Blake.

The heat seemed to fuse and become part of her being, and figments of fantasy floated in her brain. The rig lying on the all-consuming desert seemed to be a symbol of sacrifice that was like some ancient totem pole which had once demanded human life.

She tried to shut out the roaring inferno, the noise of the gusher screaming upwards, and the metallic sounds of tautened wires and groaning metal, as wreckage was hoisted to one side. Chains and tackles, lengths of drill pipes, tanks and other equipment barred her way, but then she saw Blake's tall figure directing operations. He was giving hand signals with an authority born of experience, and the oil-spattered men were all part of the fantastic tapestry as they co-ordinated his instructions.

It was difficult to discern Blake's figure from the sand. Both were covered in the black, terrible rain that soaked everyone and everything like some poisonous rash, as if it were a forerunner of some terrible disease.

Lauren tried to shout, but the roar that filled the air ate up her words. She understood now why all control was by hand signals. Coughing racked her body but, with an energy that came from some deep reserve within, she moved towards Blake.

Blood was oozing continuously from a wound in his arm, and there was a gash across his forehead where crimson streaks mingled with the oil and formed weird ridges down his face which now showed unfamiliar lines forced to the surface by pain.

'Blake,' she whispered, then cupped her hands over her mouth and yelled his name, 'Blake!', but as he turned, she drew back under the whiplash of his anger.

'What the hell are you doing here?' He pushed his breath through clenched teeth. 'I ordered you to stay put. Get back to the trailer!'

At his anger, Lauren stood petrified with disbelief, only to be brought to life again when he bellowed, 'This is no place for a woman, and I can't spare a man to take you back to Akhmar.'

The relief she had felt at seeing him unhurt evaporated, and she yelled like a fishwife, 'I thought I cared enough to see if you were safe, but don't worry, I won't make the same mistake again!'

Hot and uncomfortable, tears pricking the back of her lids, misery overwhelmed her. With dragging steps, she hobbled towards the trailer which being air-conditioned, she found was being used as a control centre.

In the desire to help, everything else was forgotten, and after drinking a cup of water which tasted like nectar from the gods, Lauren became involved in jobs which were a combination of first-aid and communications. Time ceased to have any meaning.

When darkness fell, reaction set in. The memory of Blake's features, the harshness of his words, had emptied her of all emotion. Midnight came and, from the doorway, she could see the bite of flame from the fire colour the sky, obscure the stars, and bathe everywhere in an aura of hellish unreality. Alone, she shivered, and turned to close the door, but stopped as she noticed Blake limping towards her.

The panic that had threatened to overtake her earlier now had its victory, and she rushed inside the trailer, not wanting to see Blake for even one moment. Today had somehow made his rejection of her complete, and she wanted to be away from this bitter land.

Heart beating fast, she tried to close the door, but Blake's strength pushed it open without effort.

They stood staring at each other, the silence between them almost unbearable. A sudden tightening of Lauren's throat made her aware that she was still vulnerable to his magnetism, and she became angry that she should allow herself this weakness.

For a moment, Blake stood leaning slightly back against the door-jamb, staring at her as if seeing her for the first time. His clothes were moulded to his skin by oil and sweat. The gash on his forehead was now covered by a plaster and the red scratches on either side of his face looked ugly, but they would fade. It was the scars beneath the surface that caused the trouble. The blood on his sleeve had turned a dark purple colour, and the shirt sleeve had been slit so a bandage could be placed around the wound.

The heat and the strain of the disaster had taken its toll, yet despite his exhaustion, there was still arrogance in the set of the broad shoulders which prevented her from showing sympathy.

'Well, if you aren't going to offer me iced lager on tap, at least say something,' he said.

'Such as?'

'Such as that you're glad I'm alive.'

'Of course I'm glad!' Lauren wanted to yell at him, yet despite the treacherous stirring of the old familiar emotion within her, she managed to keep her voice steady as she asked, 'Is everything over?'

'Everything is under control at this stage, if that's what you mean.'

'How long will it last?'

'Sometimes it takes weeks, even months, to put out a well fire. Experts will be called in, then we'll get the well into production. But that's in the future. For the moment...'

Blake didn't finish and, despite his arrogance, he gave

her a questing look. The expression made Lauren's foolish heart twist and turn.

'I didn't mean to get in the way,' she said. It was the nearest thing she could come to an apology. 'I only wanted to know that you were safe. After all, it's a natural reaction from a woman who loves you.' She bit on her lips. She hadn't meant to say the last few words.

The expression on Blake's face was a conflict of emotions as he moved towards her, tilting her chin with his hand.

'You choose the darnedest places to blow your top, Lauren. Who else but a firecracker like you would enact a love scene in hell let loose?'

His hand moved from her chin and touched her gently on the cheeks. 'I love you, too, but you've hardly encouraged me. Every time I seemed to be making headway, you lit the fuse. Didn't I tell you life has never been the same since you arrived on site?' He gave a semblance of his old sardonic smile. 'Even Rig Five couldn't compete. It never stood a chance. There's only one thing to do for my peace of mind——'

She looked at him quickly, hardly daring to hope. With a great effort, she played it as coolly as she could. 'Send me home, you mean?' she said. She was unable to keep a tremor from her voice.

He smiled. 'No. Your home will be here—and you'll have a ring on the appropriate finger.'

She gave a little sigh, as her heart gave a tremendous lift. 'You mean—marriage?' Even now she could hardly say it.

'That's what I was intending to convey,' he told her. For the first time he seemed to notice Lauren's dress, oil-streaked and torn and, as he studied her dishevelled appearance, there was an expression of such gentleness in his eyes that she wanted to weep.

'Pity you missed that Arab wedding,' he said, 'but attending your own should more than compensate.' He smiled. 'Let's race Kath and Ted to the altar. Never let it be said that an admin type, even a medic, could beat a desert man!' His voice became almost harsh again, as if he realised the full implications of what he was saying. 'And I am a desert man, Lauren. Always have been, always will be. You know what that means?'

'I know,' Lauren said quietly. 'Even our children will be baptised in oil.'

From the beginning, she had known the desert held her fate. It had called, and she had heard its echo, and after true Eastern tradition, it now laid claim to her, but in so doing, it had given her into the keeping of the man she loved more than anyone else in the world.

And there's still *more* love in

Harlequin Presents...

Harlequin Presents...

The beauty of true romance...
The excitement of world travel...
The splendor of first love...

What the press says about Harlequin Romances...

"...clean, wholesome fiction...always with an upbeat, happy ending."
— *San Francisco Chronicle*

"...a work of art."
— *The Globe & Mail.* Toronto

"Nothing quite like it has happened since *Gone With the Wind*..."
— *Los Angeles Times*

"...among the top ten..."
— *International Herald-Tribune.* Paris

"The most popular reading matter of American women today."
— *The Detroit News*

"Women have come to trust these clean easy-to-read stories about contemporary people, set in exciting foreign places."
— *Best Sellers*, New York

"Harlequin novels have a vast and loyal readership."
— *Toronto Star*

What readers say about Harlequin Romances

"I can't imagine my reading life without Harlequin."
J.L.,* Sioux Falls, South Dakota

"I get hours of relaxation and enjoyment reading Harlequins."
M.M., Middletown, New York

"I'm really hooked and I love it."
M.S., Richmond, Virginia

"Harlequins help me to escape from housework into a world of romance, adventure and travel."
J.R., Glastonbury, Connecticut

"I have never read a Harlequin that I did not like. They are all wonderful books."
M.H. Hatboro, Pennsylvania

"I just want you to know that I enjoy Harlequin Romances more than any book I have ever read except the Bible."

L.V., Rossville, Georgia

"I can think of no better way of relaxing than with a Harlequin. They allow me to face my world with a smile and new confidence."

L.F., Ames, Iowa

"Your books…are just what the doctor ordered."

K.B., Decatur, Georgia

"I just read my first three Harlequins. It is Sunday today, otherwise I would go back to the bookstore to get some more."

E.S., Kingston, Ontario

*Names available on request

What readers say about Harlequin Romances

"Your books are the best I have ever found."
P.B.*, Bellevue, Washington

"I enjoy them more and more
with each passing year."
J.L., Spurlockville, West Virginia

"No matter how full and happy life might be,
it is an enchantment to sit
and read your novels."
D.K., Willowdale, Ontario

"I firmly believe that Harlequin Romances
are perfect for anyone who wants to read
a good romance."
C.R., Akron, Ohio

*Names available on request